The Gypsy Piano Tuner
and
Other Romani Stories

by
Janna Eliot

Lamorna Publications

Lamorna Publications

Yew Tree Studio, Marshwood, Dorset DT6 5QF

www.lamornapublications.co.uk

First published in 2012

©Janna Eliot 2012

ISBN: 978-0-9559832-5-2

Set in 11pt Times New Roman

Contents

The artwork for the cover is by the author

Foreword

These stories, set in different times and lands, are joined by a common thread – they are all about *Romani* people. Janna Eliot touches us with the depth of her humanity. She is an able wordsmith and captures the very essence of all the varied scenes she paints. Most of the stories in this book are, in fact, based on true events, and one *senses* the reality of what she describes. Her talent for capturing dialogue is remarkable.

Romani people, indeed all Travellers, have always been marginalised, and frequently persecuted, and it is refreshing to read these stories, not written in bitterness as many could well have been, but with a moving sensitivity which allows the reader to enter to some degree into the sometimes extremely sad situations these stories reveal to us. But through it all the proud spirit of the *Romani* people shines through.

It has been my privilege to prepare these stories for publication.

Leonard Hollands

Acknowledgements

Many thanks to Sara and Derek for their support, and to Martin for his help.

Thanks also to Aad, Alexandr, Akgül, Gundula, Talip and Tulay, and to friends at Dale Farm.

I'd like to thank Leonard Hollands for publishing this book and for his sensitive and patient editing. I am so very, very grateful.

Janna

Lullaby

A cradle of smoke. A blanket of ash. A lullaby of tears.

These were Eva's first memories of childhood.

One day, a gigantic angel loomed through the mist. The khaki figure bent towards her, holding her close. Eva must have been about two at the time, though nobody was sure. The camp records had been destroyed by the fleeing Germans.

As the uniformed man lifted her into the air, Eva was engulfed by an unknown sweetness – the scent of heaven. She sniffed the brown mud he put into her hand. The mud melted and Eva licked her sticky fingers, smiling as smoothness trickled down her throat.

Later she found out the name of this sweetness. Chocolate.

There was another perfume, sharp and minty. Gum, the soldier called it. He wouldn't give her any, she remembered, in case she choked. Eva gulped in the smell as the soldier gently stroked her shaven head.

Afterwards she tried to recall his face. A sheen of black skin. Brown eyes dimmed with tears. "Holy shit!" he kept repeating. "O shit! O shit!"

Eva treasured his soft words, saved them like precious sweets.

Her next memory was of the orphanage in Czechoslovakia, a cold crumbling mansion requisitioned by the State for unclaimed children from the camps. Some of her companions were Jewish, some Gypsies, some the children of murdered political prisoners. They slept in clean beds and ate far more than they had ever eaten. They went to school. They learned to speak Czech and sing happy songs. They wore warm clothes and shoes without holes.

Eva was told that all her family had been killed. She didn't really understand what a family was. She was told she was a Gypsy. She didn't understand what a Gypsy was either. She supposed it was someone who wasn't a Jew or a Czech or the child of a political prisoner.

Sometimes, in the evening, homework and chores completed, Eva liked to sit and think by the river, beneath the flickering stars. Trees rustled and animals called from the forest. The chocolate damp earth and the crushed wild mint beneath her dress, reminded her of the soldier with the kind face and brown eyes.

"Holy shit!" she would murmur in tribute to the moon and the limitless starry sky. "O shit!"

At sixteen, Eva started work in the timber factory at Brno, and a few years later married Misha, the blond Czech stable boy who looked after the skinny horses at the orphanage. Eva felt safe in the stables, at peace with the whinnying animals and the smell of straw and manure. When she leaned her head against the neck of the huge chestnut stallion, she knew the horse understood the hollow in her life, a void so great that nothing, not even pregnancy, could fill.

The newly married couple rented a room in town, and just before the birth of their first child, Eva begged Misha to bring home slabs of chocolate. When the birth pangs began, she asked her neighbour Stefana to melt the chocolate in a large saucepan, and place the pan by the bed.

Puzzled, Stefana obeyed Eva's instructions. "Is this one of your Gypsy customs?"

Eva laughed hysterically, gritting her teeth against the pain. "Maybe! I don't know! I simply want my baby to be welcomed by the smell of sweetness."

Baby Ilana had curly black hair and dark eyes. "A Gypsy child!" Misha exclaimed in delight. Eva wept. Cradling her daughter, she wondered how her own mother must have felt, giving birth in hell.

Ilana nuzzled to her, drugged by chocolate fumes.

Stefana and the midwife were kind, but Eva longed for the mother she couldn't recall, for an aunt or sister to turn to for advice.

Ilana grew, went to school, and was suddenly an adult. There were two other children, another girl, then a boy, dark-haired and clever. All the children had long sensitive fingers like their father, and Eva's gift for singing.

Mother of three, married, a good job and friends in the timber factory; Eva's life was comfortable and settled. Yet a nameless shadow always walked at her shoulder, humming tunelessly, casting a sense of unease and guilt across her path.

Occasionally Eva read about war crimes, about the new European *Romani* Movement and demands for compensation for Holocaust victims. What good is compensation, she thought. It will only cause envy amongst my workmates. It won't bring back my murdered family.

After the Velvet Revolution in 1989, factories closed and crops failed. There were hostile glances when she joined the long lines of customers queuing for bread. There were rumours of stonings and burnings in Gypsy villages.

Eva kept her head down and tried to fit in.

The indicator showed that flight 907 from Berlin to Prague had landed. Eva stood at the Arrivals Gate, stiffening each time a child skipped through the swing doors from the luggage collection point. Then she shook her head, wincing at her stupidity.

"Lottie will be a pensioner now, even older than me!" she muttered to her daughter. Ilana squeezed her arm. Misha put his hand on Eva's shoulder, his fingers warm and comforting.

Eva studied the grey-haired passengers pushing baggage trolleys into the arrival area, stretching their cramped limbs, eyes still full of sky.

What would her sister be wearing? A long skirt and a headscarf, dangling earrings like the Romanian Gypsies who hung round Brno town square begging for money? The women who glared at her as if to say, "You may wear the clothes of a *Gadji*, but we know who you are!"

Eva had dressed carefully, rejecting the drab suits she usually wore for a calf length dress in midnight blue, and a purple jacket that skimmed her hips. Her thick greying hair was caught back in a loose chignon.

She felt her before she saw her. A striking woman with deep lines patterning a bronze face, silver hair swept up in a clip. A woman in a navy blouse and long maroon skirt.

"Eva?"

The stranger stopped in front of her, opening her arms wide, cradling Eva in a warm embrace.

The stranger whispered a stream of words into Eva's ear. "Eva! Meine Kleine, mein Liebschen, mein liebes Schwesterchen!"

Eva closed her eyes, lulled by the musical voice. Lulled by phrases she couldn't understand.

The two women swayed in each other's arms, oblivious of the photographers, the interpreter from the Red Cross International Tracing Service, the reporter from the BBC World Service.

"How did you find me?" Eva wept. "How did you know about me? It's been sixty-six years!"

She was blinded by the flash of cameras. Her hair snagged on the gold trimmings of Lottie's lacy blouse. Her heart thudded and swelled; she felt she was mumbling through a mouthful of ash.

Lottie shook her head. "Ich spreche nur Deutsch, Eva! Ich kann nicht mit Dir sprechen."

Shocked, Eva stared helplessly at Lottie. She hadn't thought about how she'd communicate with her sister. She'd assumed they'd understand each other. Tears welled in her eyes; there was so much she needed to know. She clung again to the sister lost for over half a century, grieving for a forgotten language, for an exterminated heritage.

"Holy shit!" she said in English. "O shit!"

And then, from somewhere far away, a sound vibrated. A low hum. Notes surrounded her and embraced her and mothered her.

She began to sing, a haunting melody from long, long ago. The song of the phoenix. A song of love and milk. *"Avlin Deva ...."* Was that right? The ancient *Romani* words bubbled and burst in her mouth.

Lottie clutched her hands to her chest. She joined in, her voice resonating in the airport lounge, gently correcting Eva's mistakes. *"Aldin Devla, mura sha. Ai mori shey..."*

Lottie muttered something in German, the sentence as taut and long as a string of chewing gum.

At last, the interpreter stepped forward to translate into Czech. *"Pani* Lottie says she always remembered you, her lost, beloved little sister. She's spent her life trying to find you. You were separated in the confusion, when the camp was liberated!"

Reaching for Lottie's hand, Eva said, "I never stopped wondering if I had a relative somewhere. But I was too young to remember."

Lottie spoke again.

The interpreter's eyes were full of sympathy. *"Pani* Lottie says that after the war, the Americans took her to Germany. She was fostered with a teacher's family. She had no idea you'd been sent to Czechoslovakia. And then, last month, the Red Cross told her they'd finally managed to trace you."

"The song – it's the first time I've ever remembered it – please ask her what it means."

After consulting Lottie, the interpreter turned back to Eva. "It's a lullaby. Your mother used to sing it to you both. It means, 'My sweet, my darling child, may the Lord preserve you!'"

The interpreter will go home tonight, Eva thought, and tell her husband about the two elderly Gypsies reunited by the Red Cross so many years after the end of the War. She'll fall silent, wipe her eyes and look out of the window – her husband will press her hand, then they'll finish eating their soup and dumplings, and switch on the news.

"Eva, don't you want to say something else to your sister?" asked the interpreter.

But Eva – silenced by the presence of photographers, by journalists jostling and shouting questions – didn't answer.

A camera flashed and someone called, "What does it feel like to find your sister after all these years?"

4

Eva shook her head. She wasn't going to sing for them, dance for them, tap the tambourine for them.

She brushed tears from her cheeks. In the impersonal airport lounge, the pain of her loss was keener than ever before. It was standing in front of her. A hole made flesh and blood. A stolen game, an erased possibility. A snapped string. A book with pages ripped out. A story almost at an end.

As she hugged her sister, her Lottie, Eva breathed in the scent of home.

A lullaby of tears swirled around her. *"Aldin Devla ..... mori sha...!"*

Glossary

Gadji – non-*Romani* lady (*Romani*)

Meine Kleine, mein Liebschen, mein liebes Schwesterchen. – My little, darling, beloved dear little sister. (German)

Ich spreche nur Deutsche, Eva! Ich kann nicht mit Dir sprechen. – I only speak German, Eva! I can't talk to you. (German)

Aldin Devla, mura sha. Ai mori shey... – Preserve, Lord, my daughter. Oh my child. (*Romani*)

Pani – Madam (Czech)

A Book for Naza

Naza's pitch was the big stone building. The one with three storks' nests on the roof.

Every morning, Naza left the dusty *mahala* and trekked with the other children to central Sofia. They started off before dawn, when the sky was blackish grey with a hint of rose. Sometimes they got a ride in Uncle Vanko's cart, sometimes they walked.

Naza worked with her older sister, Cherina, outside the *Biblioteka*.

"This is one of the worst pitches," Cherina complained. "We'd earn much more in the courtyard of Sveti Georgi, or outside the National Museum. When people come out of Sveti Georgi, they feel generous, because they've just been to church. And rich tourists visit the museum. Only old people and students go into the *Biblioteka*. Mainly poor people."

"But *Lelya* Elena always gives me a coin!" objected Naza. "She fumbles in her purse and says, 'Here you are, daughter, you need this more than me!' and then she smiles and wiggles her false teeth."

"She's just a shabby old woman with broken shoes!" Cherina scoffed. "She needs money more than us!"

Naza had learnt the rules of begging from Cherina. "Wait till you see someone coming towards you," Cherina had told her, "then run up to them, and start talking very quickly. Say, 'Please give me some money, I am hungry. My mother is sick. My father is far away.'" Naza had looked at Cherina in surprise. "But *Dai* isn't sick! And *Baba* isn't far away; he's got a job clearing weeds!"

Patiently, Cherina had explained. "*Baba* drinks all his money, you know that! And *Dai's* pregnant again, that's like being ill. She's sick every morning, isn't she? So we need money for our family."

Cherina showed Naza how to bow her head and look at passers-by from beneath her eyebrows. "Chase after them if they don't stop. But only follow them to the end of the road. Make sure I can see you. Make your voice high and thin, and keep saying, 'I'm hungry, please help me.' Then, if they still don't give you money, turn round at the corner and come back."

Spring was the best season for begging, with the warmth of the sun on bare legs, the soft breeze from the Vitosha mountains. People were kindest in springtime. *Lelya* Elena sometimes handed Cherina and Naza a bit of *banitsa* and they'd all sit together on the *Biblioteka* steps, chewing the fresh pastry and sucking on the cheese. In summer, the

6

sticky heat made people bad-tempered, and the water in the park fountains tasted bitter and stale.

Winter was the worst season. Then the pedestrians were bundled up in coats, their hands encased in thick gloves and their money hidden inside bags or deep pockets. Even *Lelya* Elena just smiled and apologised. "Sorry, darling, but I've spent all my money on the electric."

Naza didn't have the electric. The council didn't run cables to the Gypsy area. Some of the wealthier Roma in the *mahala* had generators, but Naza's family kept warm by huddling round the homemade stove, sitting close to each other in their tiny shack. And for light, they burnt candles when they could afford them, or made tiny lanterns from hollowed-out potatoes filled with oil.

One day, a *Gadjo* from Sofia came to the *mahala* in a black shiny car. He talked to Josef and the other leaders for a while, and in the evening, there was a meeting in the clearing. The children were chased away, but Naza and Cherina hid behind the bushes with the other kids.

Josef's voice was so loud he could be heard all over the *mahala*.

"The man who came this morning was from the Municipality," he thundered. "He says the Council want to help educate our community. They've organised a week for Roma children in Sofia *Biblioteka*. They want to take our kids to the city, show them round the library and read them stories. The visit is to be on the nineteenth of April. The man said that's International Book Day. There'll be reading workshops and sessions on story writing and how to illustrate books. A coach will be sent to transport the children to the city, and they'll be given food. Everything will be free."

"Do the kids get paid?" someone shouted. "And what's International Book Day anyway?"

"It's a trick!" yelled somebody else. "When did anyone ever do anything for us? What do our children want with reading and illustrating? Do they want to turn them back into babies?"

There was lots more talking, then Naza's father raised his voice. "We shouldn't let our children go. They'll take them away, put them in institutions, or give them to childless Bulgarians. Let the Council keep their library! We don't need it!"

Shifting to get a better view, Naza saw Big Yoni stand up. "Times are changing," Yoni said in his deep voice, looking round and spreading out his fleshy arms. "Do you want your children to be beggars forever? If our kids could read, they'd have a chance to learn about the world. They could go to school, to University even. They

7

could live in decent houses, with electricity, gas – have a chance to join the modern world."

Naza was pleased that everyone was talking about the place where she worked. "What's inside the *Biblioteka*?" she asked Cherina.

"Not sure. I think it's like a school for students and pensioners."

"Sounds boring!"

"Yes."

Their father was talking again. "And how will we manage without our children's money? Will the Council compensate us for the loss?"

"*Baba* won't let us go," sighed Cherina. "So that's that! Shame! The free food might have been really tasty! Come on, we better go for water before it gets dark."

The girls raced back to their hut, took the buckets and walked along the dusty track to the tap. By the time they'd trudged home with their pails, *Baba* was sitting at the table telling *Dai* about the meeting.

"At first we all argued. Then Josef explained the Council will pay the children to go to this Book Day, they'll get more money than they could earn in a week. So I agreed."

"I don't want to go!" Cherina objected. "I want to go begging."

"Me too," nodded Naza.

Baba wasn't listening. "Make sure you're ready early tomorrow – washed, tidy and hair combed."

That night, Naza dreamt of an enormous prison where a large white lady locked her in a cell with a book. "You will stay here until you can read!" shouted the lady, shaking a huge bunch of keys. Naza held the heavy book in her hand, staring at the marks on the page. On the table was a lump of black maggoty bread on a dirty plate.

⚜

The children on the coach were excited and a bit scared. Everyone wore their best clothes and the shoes usually saved for baptisms and weddings. They all ran up and down the vehicle, jumping on the seats until the driver yelled at them. As they jolted down the road to Sofia, Naza stared out of the window at the distant mountains.

"I don't want to spend the day inside," she said to Cherina, "I want to run after people in the street, and chat to *Lelya* Elena. She'll wonder where we are. She'll have to sit on the steps today and eat her *banitsa* all on her own."

As they drove into Sofia, the children cheered, pointing out their pitches.

"There's the church!" yelled Mitko. "Hope no one nicks my place!"

"And there's my Museum!" screeched Ema waving at an old man sitting in the dust at the kerbside. "Pavle, Pavle!" she called through the open window. The man looked up astonished as the coach drove by, then raised his crutches and grinned.

As soon as the coach stopped outside the big stone building where she begged each day, Naza jumped from the vehicle, and started to run after a well-dressed office worker. Cherina pulled her back. "Stop! We're not working today. We're going inside."

Josef was waiting for them, looking important in his black suit. The *Gadjo* who'd come to the *mahala* was with him.

"Children," said Josef, "today, you are guests of the *Biblioteka*. You must sit quietly and listen. If I hear any noise from you, I'll tell your parents. Follow me."

Naza straightened her skirt before she went into the imposing building. She'd never been inside before. She'd always felt the building was shouting at her, "Keep out! No Roma allowed!" Swallowing her fear, she followed her sister up the library steps into a long corridor. She touched one of the smooth cold walls.

She half expected someone to yell, "Go away, take your dirty hands off our clean wall!" But there was silence. Two smiling women were standing at the entrance of an enormous room. All round the walls, stacked on hundreds of shelves, were millions and millions of books. Naza stared at the bright covers of the books. She felt scared. What if she accidentally bumped into a shelf and broke it?

One of the women spoke in *Romanes*. "Come over here, dear children, and sit on the floor. My name is Lubka, and my friend here is Petya. Take a cushion and make yourselves comfortable."

Blue and orange cushions were scattered around. Cherina sat on an orange cushion, and Naza pressed beside her, comforted by the warmth of her sister's body.

"Who knows what this building is?" asked Lubka.

"The *Biblioteka*," shouted Cherina.

"Well done!" said Petya in Bulgarian. "Now, who knows what the *Biblioteka* is for?"

Naza felt proud of Cherina for answering the first question. Who would answer the second? She looked at Roberto who usually knew everything, but he sat quietly, looking at his polished shoes.

Lubka smiled. "What can you see on the shelves?"

"Books!" yelled the children.

9

"Good!" said Petya. "This is a library. A public library. That means that these books are for the people of Sofia to read. For all our citizens. Everyone is welcome to use this building – men, women and children."

She smiled. "Any questions?"

Boril whispered to Roberto. Roberto glanced at Josef, who nodded encouragingly. Roberto coughed and said, "We wondered how much it costs."

"Nothing!" laughed Petya.

Maybe she didn't understand Roberto's Bulgarian. Like all the children from the *mahala*, Roberto only spoke Bulgarian when he was begging.

Naza giggled, poking Cherina in the ribs.

Josef stood up. "It costs nothing. No money. This building is open to the public. That means everybody. Including you children."

"Including us Roma children?" Cherina was standing up, staring in amazement, and once again, Naza felt a rush of pride for her sister.

"Including you Roma children. It is for everyone."

"But we have no money to buy the books."

Naza saw tears in Lubka's eyes, and wondered if she'd hurt herself. Then Lubka leant forward, as if trying to force her words into their hearts. "You don't understand. Listen, all of you." Dramatically pointing towards the shelves, she said, "In this library there are books about everything in the world. About different places, about the sea, about music, about people who discovered new things, about different tribes and languages. There's a special section for children, with legends and tales. And you don't have to pay anything."

She held up a sheet of paper. "All you have to do is fill in a form like this with your name and address. Before you go home today, we'll give you a library card so you can borrow books. You can take books for three weeks. You don't have to pay anything."

"I can't read," Naza whispered. "I can only write my name."

In the distance she could hear someone jangling a bunch of keys. She looked round anxiously, in case the woman from her dream had come to lock her in a cell.

"What we want," Lubka went on, "is for you Roma children to learn to read and write. I understand your hard lives. I used to have a hard life too, in a *mahala* like yours. And then someone taught me to read. And once I could read, I went to school, and then to College and University. Now I work here, in this famous library in Sofia."

"I beg outside the University," shouted Rumi. "Some of the students give me money or sweets."

"Well, one day you can be a University student yourself," said Lubka. "This is the plan. If you come to the library every day after your work, some University students and library staff will teach you to read."

Naza gazed at Cherina. Her sister had a strange look on her face, as if someone had cast a spell on her.

The jangling and clinking grew louder. It was coming from the corridor. Naza stiffened, almost knocking Cherina off the cushion.

"It's the lady with the keys," she whispered. "She's going to lock us in the basement because we can't read."

The door opened and an old woman in a blue overall came in, pushing a heavy trolley laden with fruit juice and cakes. Everyone stared at the food as the trolley wobbled squeakily across the floor.

Josef stood up. "Children! You can get up now and walk around, but wait till the ladies offer you food. Remember your manners. We don't want them saying Roma children are rude and greedy."

Before they ate, Lubka took the children to the cloakroom to wash their hands. There was a washroom for girls and a washroom for boys. Naza splashed her cheeks with cold water, running her fingers through her long black hair. "One day I'll have a bathroom like this," she told Cherina, wiping her hands on a clean towel. The sisters grinned at each other in the mirror and ran back to the hall, joining their friends at the tea trolley.

After Naza had gulped down a glass of juice, Lubka took her to a table piled with colourful books. One of the covers had a picture of a Gypsy girl leading a horse to a river. Naza put her hand out to pick up the book, then hesitated, in case Lubka told her off.

"Sit down, dear," Lubka said. "Take the book."

The book felt odd, hard on the outside, its pages fanning out when she opened the cover. Naza ran her finger over the black words on the white page. Lubka took a deep breath and began reading aloud. "There was a man and he had three daughters. And he also had three sons. And one day the horse began to neigh in the pasture, because the west wind ...."

Naza laughed. "I know that story. My *Mama* tells it to me sometimes. One of the daughters is called Tsone." She recited along with Lubka. "And Tsone went to the horse and asked, "Why are you neighing so loudly?"

It was strange seeing the horse and Tsone in the pictures, and watching Lubka reading from the page. Stories came from the air, they couldn't be locked inside the covers of books.

11

Naza closed her eyes. She could see Tsone clinging to the horse's mane. She could see her galloping over the mountains. She could hear the deep voice of the wicked king. Opening her eyes, Naza stared at the shelves of books, full of secrets and stories she couldn't read, full of mysterious letters and words and sentences, magic words that could change her life.

Together, Naza and the librarian chanted the end of the story. "And I know this is true because I was there!"

Lubka smiled. "Let's fill in your form, then you can take this book home and read it yourself."

Naza frowned. Children like her didn't have books. Children like her begged outside libraries, they never went inside.

Lubka turned back to the first page. "Put your finger here, and move it along as you say the words. And that means you are reading."

For a moment Naza silently held the book to her chest, as if it was a tiny baby. Putting the book in her lap, she placed her finger on the first line. Reciting from memory, she began, "There was a man and he had three daughters."

This is my first book, she thought. A book for Naza.

Glossary

mahala – an area of town where Romanies live   (*Romani*)

Biblioteka – library   (Bulgarian)

Dai – mother   (*Romani*)

Baba – father   (*Romani*)

Lelya – aunt   (*Romani*)

banitsa – a type of pastry   (Bulgarian)

Gadjo – non-*Romani* man   (*Romani*)

Romanes – *Romani* language   (*Romani*)

Mama – Granny   (*Romani*)

The Piano Tuner of Delft

He'd been asleep in his trailer.

Somewhere in the distance, a trumpet was playing – low, insistent, throbbing. Then the sound turned into the chugging of a car. A door slammed. Someone shouted his name.

"This can't be happening again!" Niko groaned. "Not now. Not in our modern times."

His heart thudded painfully as he waited for the door to fly open. But the wood didn't splinter. The hinges didn't sob. No one came crashing in to haul him out of bed. There was only a soft insistent tapping on the window and a hoarse whisper. "Niko, *oude vriend*, wake up! Please! We need you!"

With a grunt, Niko pulled himself up and staggered to the window. Peering out, he saw Piet, his old friend from town, shivering in the May dawn. Niko shuddered. It had been another May morning, over half a century ago, when the others had come, uniformed and shouting, dragging his family from their beds and forcing them out into the cold spring day.

Eyes blurred with sleep, Niko fumbled with the door. "Come in, Piet," he croaked. "What is it?"

Slipping off his shoes, Piet eased himself into the rickety chair. "Please, Niko, Delft needs you! How long will it take you to get ready?"

Niko focussed on Piet's socks. They were made of soft black wool, not like his own mismatched pair. A married man's socks, he thought, wiping moisture from his eyes.

"Give me fifteen minutes, but first, tell me what you want? And why me? I'm an old man now, what can I do?"

"The guy we booked to tune the piano in the town square was rushed to hospital last night. Appendicitis! Imagine, what bad timing! Just before the fifth of May, Liberation Day."

Niko frowned. "And you can't find anyone else in the whole of Delft to tune your piano, only me?"

Piet shrugged. "There are hardly any piano tuners left, Niko! Who buys real pianos these days? It's all electronic keyboards and computers now. You're one of the few people left who *can* tune a piano!"

Niko filled a basin from the tap outside his trailer and washed his face. His hands trembled slightly as he shaved, squinting at himself in the mirror on the trailer wall.

"And where were the citizens of Delft when us Sinti needed *them*?" he mumbled to himself.

He bent his head, wiping the foam off his chin. There had been some brave people like Piet's father, willing to hide Gypsies and Jews in cellars and attics. But they'd all been betrayed and caught anyway.

They drove to town in silence. Holiday traffic clogged the roads – decorated floats, visitors from outlying hamlets, lorries carting produce for the restaurants. Everyone was driving towards Delft for the Liberation Day Celebrations.

Piet offered him a Stuyvesant, and they lit up, grey wisps of smoke curling at the car windows. Sunk in his seat, Niko thought back to his own liberation day, when the prisoners in the camp had been freed.

"I still remember the cheap cigarettes the Russian Army handed out," he muttered, "and later, the rich food the Americans offered us, which made us sick!"

With Sonja, his only remaining relative, Niko, then eleven years old, had hitched back to the family trailer site in Zuid-Holland and tried to rebuild his life. A few other Gypsies straggled back to the old encampment. But life was never the same again, not like before the war. The pain was too deep.

It was Piet's father, Aad, who'd arranged Niko's apprenticeship with a piano tuner. Niko found consolation in tuning pianos. There was a structure, something he could control. Life was the opposite, a series of random events, sometimes happy, mostly catastrophic. A piano was an instrument with logic. Going up the keyboard the notes got higher, going down the notes got lower.

Notes went out of tune of course – after a piano had stood neglected for years in a barn, or after extreme swings in temperature, like in the frosty *hongerwinter* of 1944. But a swift turn of the tuning wrench adjusted the pitch, and all was right again.

If only life was like that, thought Niko, as a huge lorry overtook them, shaking Piet's car. If only we could blow away the dust of history, tweak the tuning tool and turn it till the notes rang true. But how do you fix what happened back then, in the war? How do you forget the screams of the slaughtered? How can you dispel the shadows?

As they approached the city, Piet relaxed his grip on the steering wheel.

"*Ja, ja!*" he said. "Thank you, Niko. You know the whole town will turn out this afternoon to celebrate. And a pianist from the Amsterdam *Concertgebouworkestra* is coming to play for us. They're bringing the piano over this morning. We'll pay you for the tuning, of course, and give you lunch. With as much as you want to drink!" He laughed and added, "After you've finished, *naturlijk!*"

Turning into the drive of a neat whitewashed house, Piet sounded the horn and switched off the engine. "But first, we'll have a good breakfast. Lottie's cooking *pannenkoeken*."

Lottie, Piet's wife, opened the door, standing on tiptoe to kiss Niko's cheek. "Welcome, dear friend! So long since we last met. Who'd have thought that Piet would be in charge of the arrangements for this year's celebrations, and that you'd be tuning the piano? Big shots!"

Niko was seated at the table with a plate of ham, cheese, and soft bread. The smell of freshly ground coffee wafted in from the kitchen, catching at the back of his throat. Niko had never married, and his sister had only survived a few months after the war. With Sonja's death, the world had become even bleaker, enclosing him in a realm of fog and shadows, shrouding him from normal life. So he had thrown himself into work, going round houses, schools and concert halls, tuning pianos. At night, after a simple meal in his trailer, he tiredly fixed himself a mug of cheap instant coffee.

Lottie poured the rich brew into a porcelain cup. Warming his hands on the elegant china, Niko glanced round the room. Framed photographs of Piet and Lottie's family were ranged over the cabinet. Niko swallowed hard, forcing down a mouthful of ham. The pancake lay half-eaten on his plate.

Bitter anger surged through him for the years the Nazis had stolen, and he choked. Lottie placed her warm hand over his. "This is such a difficult day," she said. "We all lost so much..."

Looking down, Niko realised the cuff of his shirt had ridden up, exposing the faded blue numbers on his arm. He pulled down his sleeve, hiding the marks.

They took a taxi to the *Stadhuis*. Outside the magnificent civic building, a striped awning had been erected to shield the grand piano. Niko unwrapped his tools, spreading them out on a green baize cloth. He flexed his fingers, preparing for his task.

"I'll be back at lunchtime to see how you're getting on," promised Piet. "I have to go now to check the other arrangements."

The awning reminded Niko of the tent he'd slept in as a boy in summer, when relatives from other encampments had come to visit. Smiling, he struck his tuning fork on the stool. The metal vibrated, giving out a low hum.

The inside of the piano smelt of musky secrets, loves and passions. He adjusted the keys of the middle octave, but one pin stubbornly refused to move. He soaked his rag in oil and draped it over the tuning pin, leaving it for a few seconds. When the pin moved freely up and down, he played a few chords and nodded. The middle notes were sound. A gang of children who'd gathered by the stage clapped, calling out, "Bravo!" Niko turned and smiled. He loved children.

"Maybe it's lucky I didn't bring kids into this evil world, to see them ruthlessly snuffed out like diseased chickens!" he muttered. He closed his eyes to blot out the memory of his little brother being dragged screaming to the place of smoke and ash.

Looking up from the keys, he slowly massaged his neck, relaxing his strained shoulder muscles. The square was filling with visitors. Stallholders exchanged jokes with customers, children ran by with balloons. Niko straightened his back as a group of old men walked by. For them, like him, this wasn't a celebration. It was a wake, a jangled memory. His fingers ached and he fanned them out, remembering how his cousin used to make the same movement before playing the violin.

Suddenly the square was full of sweet music, and a little boy stood before him, playing a haunting melody.

Niko blinked. "Is that you, Willy?" Blinded by tears, he answered himself in a low voice. "No, cousin, you are only a memory." The violinist sweeping a bow across the fiddle was just another young boy, another outcast from a modern war, a victim of modern prejudice. Above the boy's head fluttered a banner reading, '60 jaar Bevrijding. Vrij Delft viert feest.'

When Niko started on the higher octaves, the notes trilled and trembled like butterflies and larks. Like stardust.

There remained only the lowest notes to tune. These were always the hardest to adjust, with their underlying threatening bass, their menacing power.

Niko gave a final twist with the wrench, dusted off the strings and lowered the huge upper lid, polishing the mahogany cover so it gleamed in the sun. Then, as a final check, he played the piano tuner's melody he'd adapted from an old children's song, a tune which used every note on the keyboard.

He was alone beneath the awning, just him and the beautiful instrument. The notes gushed out of him, astonishing him with their passion, ringing across the square and rising into the sky. He heard Willy harmonising, adding riffs and trills, as together they played the beautiful ancient Sinti melody.

Applause thundered over the square. I must be dreaming, he thought, as he stood up. As he left the stage he was met by cheers and smiling faces, by clapping hands and approving whistles. Piet bustled up. "That was fantastic, *oude vriend*, thank you so much. A lovely melody. The Town Council really appreciates you saving the day."

Niko followed Piet to an open-air bar in the square, where he ordered chips and sausages, washed down with Pils. As he ate, customers smiled and clapped him on the shoulder. The waitress came out with more bottles of beer and a plate of *poffertjes*. "On the house, compliments of the manager!"

Niko's mouth watered at the sight of the sweet light pastry filled with cream. It had been years since he'd tasted a *poffertje*. Just before Holland had been occupied in May 1940, his mother had brought him into town to sell pegs and brass ornaments. When their baskets were empty, she'd bought him a *poffertje*. The pastry was sugary with the promise of the future, coated in white icing powder which tickled the back of his throat like a secret giggle.

Smiling, Niko picked up the cake. As he breathed in the smell of the past, the white dusting on the *poffertje* made him choke.

Glossary

oude vriend – old friend   (Dutch)

hongerwinter – winter of hunger (1944, when starving Dutch people ended up eating tulip bulbs)   (Dutch)

concertgebouworkestra – philharmonic orchestra   (Dutch)

naturlijk – of course, naturally   (Dutch)

Stadhuis – town hall   (Dutch)

65 jaar Bevrijding. Vrij Delft viert feest – 65 years since the Liberation. Free Delft celebrates   (Dutch)

poffertje – tiny pancake dusted with icing sugar   (Dutch)

Notes from the London Underground

An iron stairway spiralled downwards into darkness. Jerry hesitated, resting his accordion on the peeling railing as he peered into the gloom.

The man in front of him stumbled on the first step, clutching the metal banister to regain his balance. The trombone he'd been carrying clanged down the steps and disappeared into the shadows, landing far below with a ringing thud.

Jerry grasped the straps of his accordion tighter and picked his way down the awkward stairs.

William, the interviewer from SubLondon Sounds, stood at the bottom of the stairs, holding out the trombone. Returning the instrument to its owner, he led the musicians towards a long wooden platform bench. "Wait here, everybody. We'll start in a few minutes."

The musicians were in a musty, disused tunnel. Jerry positioned his accordion on his knee, comforted by its familiar weight. The trombonist anxiously examined his instrument, puffing into the mouthpiece.

"No damage done!" he said. "Wonder how many judges there are."

"I kind of imagined four, like X Factor," Jerry replied.

"Please, not Simon Cowell!" The blonde with the cello wiped imaginary sweat from her forehead and flapped her hand, teeth gleaming in a smile.

William reappeared, holding a clipboard and a pencil. "Miss Arnold," he called. "If you'd like to come through."

The girl shook her hair, whispered, "Wish me luck," and picked up her large instrument. Jerry watched her walk round the corner into the gloom.

"Looks like a racehorse with an overweight jockey," the trombonist laughed.

The sound of an Elgar concerto floated round the tunnel, transforming the dingy catacomb into a realm of light and gold. Jerry leant back on the hard bench, transported to a land of palm trees and gentle seas. "She's good!" he murmured.

"Yeah," grunted the trombonist. "Royal School of Music, I bet. You can always clock the posh kids. They always get a pitch. Don't seem fair really, not when people like me really need a job."

Jerry fidgeted nervously. He wasn't a posh kid. He'd learned the accordion from his Dad, picked up tunes at fairs, had a few lessons with Les, the old man who'd pitched his caravan down the allotments for a couple of years – till the Council moved him on.

The tune stopped abruptly in the middle of a bar, and the girl returned, bent beneath her cello.

William reappeared with his clipboard. "Mr. Atkins?" The trombonist patted his instrument and stood up. "Good luck!" chorused the other applicants as he went into the shadowy vault.

The cellist slackened her bow, and manoeuvred her instrument into its cloth case. "The zip's broken," she explained, tugging at the fastening. "I have to do it up with these massive kilt pins." Jerry laughed and got up to help, stabbing a pin into the thick sacking.

"How do you manage to get around with this?" he asked. "It must be so heavy for you. You're so small and slender."

He bit his lip. He sounded like he was hitting on her.

The girl grinned. "I'm tougher than I look. Working on a farm as a kid developed my muscles."

She winced as discordant notes howled along the tunnel. After a couple of bars the noise stopped and the trombonist reappeared. "I think they liked me," he smiled.

Jerry felt sick. Sweat broke out on his forehead. He'd been so busy dreaming about palm trees and gentle seas, he hadn't twigged the girl had just played his audition piece. The piece he'd adapted for accordion and been practising for weeks – Elgar's Cello Concerto. He couldn't play it now, not after she'd performed it so beautifully. It would sound naff on the accordion after that.

The girl leaned forward. "What's up? You've gone really pale."

Jerry took a deep breath. "Your audition piece – that's what *I* was gonna do. My mind's gone blank. I can't think of anything else to play."

"Sorry," the girl said, but she didn't look very apologetic. "You must know something else. Beethoven? *Ode to Joy?*"

"Yeah, I could play that." Unclipping the accordion, he released the bellows, making soft puffs, riffing up the keyboard. Was it G sharp or G flat. He'd have to trust to luck, improvise a bit.

A few minutes later, the drummer was ushered through the dark into the audition area and dull thuds echoed round the passage. The rapping began slowly, then speeded up, driving pellets of sound into the stone floor and walls. The noise built to a deafening crescendo, then fell away into quick rhythmic clicks. At first it sounded like the threatening knocks of *gavvers* pounding on the door, then like rain on a trailer roof.

Transported back to childhood, Jerry saw Ma's pale face in the lantern light, as a policeman thrust an eviction order into her hands. Battered by weariness, she pleaded for a bit more time. "Let us stay till mornin', officer, so the kids can have a bit of sleep and a bite to eat afore we go."

Now there was an unrelenting thudding, like the blows of bullies beating up a child. "Lowlife! Caravan trash!" Jerry rubbed his hand across his face, feeling long faded bruises and cuts. His heart speeded up, racing with the drum.

Silence. The drummer reappeared through the gloom, blinking in the fluorescent light. "Did it sound okay?" he asked anxiously.

"Fine," everyone assured him, ears ringing from the sound assault.

The blonde had finally packed up her enormous cello. She smiled at Jerry. "Nervous?"

"Yeah! A bit. I really need to pass this audition. I jacked in my job last week. I'm kind of following a dream, but I'm not sure I'm good enough to get a busker's licence."

"Want me to wait with you? We could grab a coffee after and compare notes." She laughed, "Literally!"

Jerry nodded. "Notes from the Underground! Thanks, that'd be good."

"No probs. My name's Julie."

"Jerry," he answered, holding out his hand. "Nice to meet you."

It had been a long time since anyone had taken an interest in him, and he felt awkward and embarrassed. And very, very pleased.

William reappeared. "Miss Markovitz, come with me." The violinist picked up her bow and started to play, marching round the corner in time to rousing music. The tune stopped abruptly and a sobbing Tchaikovsky melody soared to the sooty ceiling. Jerry blinked. He saw his father's face, worn out with winters and the constant *jalling* on. The music mourned and lamented, drenching him with sadness. He groaned.

"You'll be fine," Julie told him. "The auditioners are really nice."

"Are you at music school?" Jerry asked.

"Yes, part timer at The Royal College of Music. I'm on a scholarship, but it's not enough to live on, and my folks are tenant farmers and can't help. I've been working as a vet's assistant so I can pay the bills and buy new strings and so on. But I still can't make ends meet. They say that on a good day, you can make loads of money busking. If I get my busker's licence, I'll be able to practice on the job

20

– I can't really play much in my digs – disturbs the landlady!"

The violinist returned. "That was brilliant!" Jerry told her. "You're a beautiful player."

"Thank you," said the lady, in a heavy East European accent. "I have not played for so long, it is a pleasure for me. The acoustics here are very excellent." She placed her instrument gently back in its case. "Now I must go, but I wish you all you best of the luck."

The flautist was called in, his flute dull silver in the dim light. The tunnel filled with swooping joyous notes like the call of a bird at twilight. Jerry gripped his accordion tighter. His throat was burning and dry. "I could murder a strong cuppa with three sugars," he muttered.

Two more people to go. A young lad with a banjo, and himself. Jerry wiped his sweaty hands on his jeans, hoping he was next.

But the banjo player was called in. Jerry hummed along as the notes of *When I'm cleaning windows* wafted through the air. The song took him back to when he was thirteen, cleaning windows with Dad after they'd pulled in on the common near Riversend. Most of the old people in the hamlet welcomed them, filling buckets with warm soapy water, bringing out cups of coffee and slabs of homemade cake. Most of them. There was always the odd nasty one, like that Major Brown who threatened to turn his dogs on them. "If I had my way, you'd all be sent back to India! Scroungers and beggars, the lot of you!"

Quick footsteps clattered down the iron stairway, and a man with a guitar stumbled into the tunnel. "Have I missed it? Am I too late? There was a signal failure…."

Anxiously, he opened his guitar case. "Can you give me an E, mate?" he asked Jerry.

For a moment Jerry didn't understand. "An E? I don't do drugs!"

The guitarist laughed and pointed at the accordion. "No, pal! I mean top E. To tune up."

Jerry grinned and played a soft note. The guitarist adjusted his strings.

When I'm cleaning windows came to an end, and the interviewer came round the corner with his list. "Is Pedro Peters here yet?"

The guitarist crossed himself and followed William into the shadows.

"I made a mistake in the second verse," the banjo player said. "I played it perfectly at home, but I cocked it up when it really mattered."

"They probably thought you were improvising," Julie said comfortingly.

The warm rich notes of the guitar transported Jerry to Seville, to the summer his sister Betty-Ann had married an Andalusian Gypsy. He could feel the warm sun on his face, smell the orange blossom.

Someone was jabbing his ribs. "Your turn," Julie hissed. "William's waiting. Good luck!"

'This is it,' Jerry thought, swinging his accordion onto his shoulders. Trying to look confident, he followed William through the gloomy passage.

Three judges were sitting behind a table, pens poised over paper sheets. "Hello," smiled the woman. "Sorry to have kept you waiting. What are you going to play?"

"I'll start off with a bit of Beethoven, then some Gypsy tunes!"

The interviewers looked at each other. "Interesting!" said William. "When you're ready."

Jerry opened the bellows, letting air gush into the accordion. He felt his instrument come alive, impatient to gallop through the music. He swung into *Ode To Joy*, embellishing it with flourishes and giving it a Balkan beat.

The adjudicators tapped their feet, nodding their heads in time. He sensed he had them. He swung into a lament, making the accordion wail and weep. "Born in the middle of the afternoon, in a horsedrawn waggon on the old A5..." His voice was deep with ancient rejections. "Move along, get along! Go, move, shift!"

He wondered if he should stop, but the adjudicators gestured him to continue. *"Dordi, dordi, dik akai,"* Jerry continued, changing to a major key and swinging into the familiar children's rhyme. He knew he'd get his licence, that his life would change forever.

Julie was waiting for him. They'd grab a coffee and compare notes from the Underground.

Glossary

gavvers – policemen (Anglo-*Romani*)

jalling on – moving on (Anglo-*Romani*)

yog – fire *(Romani)*

dordi, dordi, dik akai – dearie, dearie, look (over) here (Anglo-*Romani*)

The Dream Job

Lena yawns, picks up the bucket and tugs open the door of the shack. A breeze shivers across the rubbish heap, over the cans littering the field.

She walks sleepily to the well, eyes half shut against the rising sun. Her friend Melia is already pumping the handle of the well up and down. Silver gouts of water gush into the pail.

The day continues like all the other days. Zhenia swaggers by with a bundle of twigs. Viktor chases chickens. Men sit outside huts, repairing cars or old furniture. Women stoop over washtubs, scolding children. Dogs bark.

Suddenly everything stops. A limousine is chugging up the track. As it shudders to a halt, two figures climb out. Lena recognises her cousin Valdi, but the other man is a stranger. The tip of his cigar is a copper glow, snaking silver smoke into the sky. "This is Eduard," Valdi says as the villagers crowd round.

Eduard has a wide smile. He speaks in a deep film star voice, his gold teeth flashing promises. "I'm looking for workers. I've come to offer your children a dream job. In London, at the Hilton Hotel. Translating for rich Eastern European guests. Wonderful pay and conditions, massive tips, lots of opportunities."

The villagers' eyes glitter with hope and greed. A tray is passed round and Eduard accepts a drink and hands out cigarettes. The tarnished tray and the glasses glint in the sunlight, hypnotising Lena with their brightness. Entranced, she stares at this man who has come to lead her to a better life.

"Only the cleverest children are suitable," Eduard continues. "The Hilton needs young people aged between fifteen and twenty. I'll sort out contracts, provide passports. Get them free English lessons. All those chosen will receive new clothes."

A few parents mutter to each other. Valdi glares at them. "Listen to Eduard! He's doing us a great honour, picking our Roma children. He could have chosen Ukrainian or Russian kids from the town, but he wants *our* youngsters because they learn quickly."

Eduard glances at the gold watch on his wrist. "I don't have much time. Bring the children over here. I will choose the best."

Lena feels her mother's bony fingers prodding her spine. "Don't slouch!" her mother commands. "Smooth back your hair! Smile! Try to look intelligent. You're almost fifteen! You have the chance to go abroad, to London. And you know how much we need money."

Shyly, Lena walks across the scrubby grass, praying Eduard will choose her. "He's sure to take us," she whispers to Melia. "We're the cleverest children in the settlement. We were top of the class until we had to leave school!"

Eduard looks the assembled adolescents up and down, staring at their bodies, pointing to those he finds suitable.

"Stand in front of the tree if I call your name," shouts Valdi. Lena fixes her eyes on Eduard, willing him to point at her. He picks Zhenia. He takes Mara and Tanyita. Lena holds her breath. She looks over to Eduard's Mercedes, at the light bouncing off the wing mirror. Valdi calls her name.

A warm glow spreads through her. She is one of the chosen. She's going to London to work as a translator. She waits for Eduard to point at Melia. Everyone knows how clever Melia is. Melia is wearing a long brown skirt and a dark red blouse, her hair pulled back in a tight bun. She's just put on the broken glasses she keeps in her pocket, and looks very sensible, much cleverer than Zhenia or Tanyita. Melia's family worked in Warsaw for three years, so she can speak Polish as well as *Romani* and Ukranian.

But Eduard is already walking away. "What about Melia?" Lena shouts. "She's the cleverest of us all." Valdi shakes his head and makes a fist. "He has chosen. Be quiet, or you'll lose your place."

That night there's a farewell party. "Why didn't he choose any young men?" asks Viktor's father.

"He doesn't trust boys," Valdi explains. "Boys go off on their own and take up with loose women. Girls are the best workers."

It's midnight. The summer moon is huge and golden. Eduard drives up in a camper van, and families gather round. Lena hugs her mother tightly, kisses her brothers and sisters goodbye. Excitement turns to a nagging ache.

Her mother hangs a tiny cross woven from straw and red thread round Lena's neck. "Be good. Keep safe. May God grant you a safe journey."

Melia stands at the back of the crowd, holding her patched-up glasses in her hand. Her loose hair streams across her shoulders. She looks beautiful. She waits till Eduard is speaking to Valdi, then darts across to say goodbye, knotting a handmade bracelet round Lena's arm.

The eleven young women climb into the van. It's the first time Lena has ever left her family. Her face is wet with tears. Her mother is howling. Everyone's sobbing, even Zhenia. A pack of dogs surrounds the car, yelping mournfully.

Eduard starts the engine and calls out of the window. "You parents should be rejoicing, not weeping! With the money your girls will send back, you'll be able to buy new apartments in Kiev!"

Tanyita grips Lena's arm. Lena stares out of the window. They jolt down the potholed track to the tarmac road then Eduard races the van along the highway. Lena laughs. She's only ever travelled in Marko's old truck; this new camper van is a magic carpet whisking her to glory.

"I was sure they'd choose Melia," she says. "She's the brightest girl in the settlement."

Zhenia laughs. "You're so thick! Did you really think they'd pick an ugly mare like her?"

"She's not ugly!" protests Lena. "She's got beautiful eyes and her skin's smooth as water. And Eduard wants clever people!"

"Why did he pick you, then?" demands Zhenia. "You can't even figure out what's going on! You're so dim! I'm only here to find my sister."

"What do you mean? Your sister's working in Hollywood. Everyone knows that! Your mother's always boasting about her!"

Tanyita is staring out of the window, tears rolling down her cheeks. Lena takes her hand. "Don't worry," she soothes. "We'll be alright. We'll make loads of money in London. We'll eat the finest food and sleep in warm, soft beds."

One by one, her companions fall asleep. Lena looks out of the window at the shadowy trees, at villages wrapped in night. A deer stares from a field, eyes bright in the moonlight.

Lena wonders what people eat in England. She realises she doesn't know anything at all about England, apart from the fact there's a Queen. Or is it a King? She doesn't know any English, not one word. But Eduard will arrange English lessons for the Roma girls so they can translate for the rich Eastern European guests.

The van jolts to a halt at a checkpoint and Eduard gets out to talk to the guards. He passes over a packet and a couple of bottles and the soldiers smile and laugh, lifting the barrier.

As the van crosses the frontier, Lena dozes, her head on Tanyita's shoulder. When she wakes, it's late morning. She wipes her eyes and gazes out of the window. Everything looks different. Her back is aching and her stomach is as hollow as an empty pot.

"Welcome to Slovakia," Eduard says, swinging the van into a dense forest. The girls get out and stretch their legs. They wash their faces in a little brook and Eduard hands round baskets of food. The girls laugh and sing, spreading a tablecloth over the grass and setting out rolls and sausages and cheese. Mara hums a tune and Tanyita starts to dance.

Laughing, Lena joins in, the moss springy beneath her feet. Eduard looks at his watch. "Okay, girls, time to move. We've a long drive before us."

The sun shines through the dark leaves of the trees. Lena spots a hollow oak, and is tempted to climb into its cool shelter and hide. If I go now, she thinks, I can find my way back home. I'll just keep walking south.

Then she remembers why she's in this forest, far away from her family. She's going to be a translator and make loads of money. She's going to buy her parents a new brick house so they can leave their hut with its leaking tin roof and the door that always sticks. She'll get the best medicine for her brother Stefan, so he'll stop coughing. She'll buy cousin Rika a wheelchair, one of those motorised ones rich people use. Rika is so sweet, but has to struggle around on the rough wooden crutches Valdi made her.

It's hot in the van, and the air is stale. Lena tries to stay awake, she wants to see all the new places they're passing so she can tell her family about them when they meet again. But Eduard lights a cigar, and the pungent smoke forces her to close her eyes. When she wakes, the light seems less intense, the air thicker. The houses are grey and tall.

"You girls have been asleep for hours," Eduard says. "We're in Austria."

Night falls. They're in a large town, driving past huge shops in brightly lit streets. At last Eduard stops outside a hotel. "See how I look after you?" he smiles. "We'll have something to eat here, you can wash and I'll give you the new clothes I promised."

"New clothes!" Lena giggles, pinching Tanyita as they clamber out of the van and follow Eduard into the hotel. Upstairs, there are five bunks in a small room, with a couple of mattresses on the dusty floor. Lena puts her little case on a top bunk. A fat woman with dyed red hair shows them a dirty bathroom. The girls look at each other in surprise. They try the taps and laugh when rusty water comes out. Tanyita finds a cloth and cleans the filthy sink, wipes the cracked toilet seat.

"Come on!" Eduard calls. "Food's ready."

The girls wash their hands. Lena lets the brown water run through her fingers, then follows her friends down to a large room where bowls of soup and chunks of fresh bread are served. The soup smells lovely. Lena eats quickly, warmth spreading through her body.

Eduard is in a good mood. Finishing his coffee, he calls for beer. When the waitress returns with his drink, he slaps her rump and she laughs.

Lena looks at Tanyita, and they snigger behind their hands. They've all heard stories about how the *Gadje* behave.

Eduard leaves the room, returning with a case. When he snaps open the lid, Lena sees the gleam of silk. He gives out clothes and shoes. "Take these upstairs, girls, try them on. Comb your hair and tidy yourselves. You must look your best for the clients."

In the dormitory, the girls examine their garments. Lena peels off her long shabby skirt and loose blouse. The black silk dress skims her knees, the bodice is cut low. She knows her mother wouldn't approve, she'd purse her lips, tossing her head.

"Lena! Stop squeezing your lips together," Zhenia laughs. "Smile, you look really pretty!"

In the corner of the cramped room there's a wardrobe with a full-length mirror. Lena has never seen herself in a long mirror before. A tall, thin girl with long black hair and golden earrings looks back at her. She smirks at her elegant dress, her brown legs, the shiny high-heeled purple shoes. This must be what they call the English chic. The shoes really pinch, but they look lovely.

She tucks the cross her mother gave her under her bodice.

Tanyita is wearing a tiny bolero and a shiny red skirt. When she bends to pull the skirt over her knees, her bolero gapes open.

Eduard is calling again. "Time for the fashion show!" he yells. Stumbling downstairs, Lena follows her friends back to the dining room. It's hard to keep upright in her uncomfortable shoes and she leans against Zhenia for support. Zhenia scowls but doesn't move away.

The fat landlady and a man in a striped suit are sitting next to Eduard, talking in German. The man has a notepad in front of him.

"Okay, girls," Eduard smiles. "Good news for some of you. I've just got a message from the manager of the Hilton Hotel. They don't need as many translators as they thought, so some of you will be staying here instead. Same rates of pay and same conditions. You'll be closer to home. Tomorrow, you'll move to a newly decorated annexe reserved for top guests. The paint isn't quite dry, so you'll stay here tonight."

Lena looks at Zhenia. Zhenia scowls. Eduard calls out five names, including Tanyita's. Tanyita is so busy trying to cover her chest and legs with her tight clothing, she doesn't hear what Eduard is saying.

"Tanyita, you've been chosen to stay here, in Austria," Lena whispers. "You're lucky. You'll be able to visit home easily."

Despite her words, Lena is sorry for Tanyita. Her friend has missed out on the chance to go to England.

No one sleeps much. The beds are dirty and smelly, and Lena feels sick. She thinks about her family. She wonders who is helping her mother. She hopes her little sister is strong enough to wash the clothes and collect firewood. For a moment, she wishes she was safe at home.

She reminds herself how lucky she is. Going to London. To a dream job working in a high-class hotel, translating for rich East European guests. Wonderful pay and living conditions, massive tips, lots of opportunities.

In the morning, she kisses Tanyita goodbye. "Don't cry! You'll be fine. The other girls will look after you. We'll see each other soon."

Smiling, she follows Zhenia down to the van. She's nearly fifteen years old, and this is the most exciting thing that's ever happened to her. Thanks to Valdi, she's going to London. She's going to be rich. She'll meet film stars and rock stars. A wave of emotion and gratitude sweeps over her. She imagines cousin Rika zooming about in a shiny new wheelchair. She pictures her parents waving from the doorway of their modern brick house, a house with new beds and a bathroom with running water. When she goes back to visit, the whole settlement will run out with flowers and cakes to welcome her. She'll drive up in a red Mercedes, and throw money and sweets from the car window.

Soft drizzle weeps on her hair. At the corner of the street, a woman in a long flowered dress stands outside a shop, staring at the van with dull eyes. She's selling magazines.

Zhenia gasps and smothers a scream.

Accustomed to Zhenia's dramatic ways, Lena climbs into the van. There's more space now so the girls spread themselves out, slipping off their uncomfortable new shoes and resting their feet on the spare seats. They are waiting for Eduard and Zhenia to get in.

Suddenly there's a scream from the pavement. Lena looks out of the window. Eduard is tugging Zhenia's hair, then he slaps her. Blood pours from Zhenia's nose. The door opens and Zhenia is thrown into the van. Eduard gets into the driver's seat, slamming the door.

Lena comforts her friend, staunching the blood with her scarf, hugging her tightly. "What's the matter, Zhenia? Why did you try to run away? Don't you want to go to London?"

Zhenia points at the figure weeping near the shop. The woman has dropped her magazines, and is slumped on the ground. Her arms are stretched towards the car. She is screaming to Zhenia. Zhenia mumbles through swollen lips and presses her bruised fingers to the window. The engine throbs and they drive off.

Lena touches the straw cross at her neck, twists the handmade bracelet on her wrist.

"We're going to London. A dream job, working at the Hilton. To translate for rich East European guests. Wonderful pay and living conditions, massive tips, lots of opportunities."

Glossary

Gadje – non-*Romani* people (*Romani*)

The Kid from Sulukule

It was Ahmet's seventh birthday.

He was woken by the smell of cardamom and coffee and the rumble of low voices from the kitchen. Creeping from the bed he shared with Hakim, he tiptoed to the bead curtain and listened.

His mother was weeping as she kneaded dough. "Our people have lived here for generations! Where will we go? Why are they doing this to us? Is it because we are *Romanlar*, or because we're poor?"

Grandfather cleared his throat. "They're just trying to frighten us. They won't do anything. Nothing's going to happen. You'll see."

Ahmet pushed through the curtain and ran to his mother. Her tears dropped onto the *pitta* dough, while Grandfather calmly continued preparing coffee.

"Why is my mother crying? Why are you frightened?"

Grandfather gave the *ibrik* a final swirl and poured coffee into glasses. "Your mother is crying because you are so grown up now!"

Lowering himself onto a cushion, the old man pointed to the wooden casket on the floor.

"Ahmet, my precious grandson. This is your birthday gift from me. When I was seven, my own grandfather gave me this casket. Today, I'm an old man, and *you* are seven. So I'm passing it on to you.'

Grandfather opened the box, releasing the sharp smell of polish. He coughed and spoke again. "Take care of these tools, my boy, with these you will make money for the family."

Ahmet nodded. He felt different from yesterday, more important, taller, stronger. He was a man. He was starting work. Tonight there would be a party.

The sun was just rising as Ahmet, face washed, black curls combed, wearing a patched white shirt and his father's cut down trousers, followed the other boys along the narrow paths of Sulukule. From every house came the sound of shouting and laughter, with music blaring from radios. Neighbours were waving from windows, calling to friends across the street.

Hakim was carrying a wooden foot-mount and a light camping stool. Proudly holding his heavy box, Ahmet followed his brother down the alley. The casket banged against his thigh as he walked, and the Sulukule girls teased him, dancing and laughing. Amina, his neighbour, squealed out, "Hail, the mini-hero! The little shoeshine boy with such a big casket! How many shoes will he clean today?"

Her shrill voice mingled with the call of gulls from the port.

Hakim chased Amina away, pretending to shove the camping stool into her face. "Clear off, or I'll scrub your dirty mouth with my brush!" Still jeering, Amina ran past, swinging her bright skirt.

As they turned into the cobbled lane, Ahmet heard a rumbling. The street shook as three bulldozers, groaning and screeching like angry monsters, shuddered up the narrow track. The children flattened themselves against the wall as the vehicles squeezed by.

"Where are you going?" Hakim called to one of the drivers.

"*Öğreneceksin oğlum.* You'll find out soon enough, my lad!" the man answered sullenly.

Ahmet hurried to keep up with the older boys, hoisting his box higher as he stumbled down the alleys. By the time the children reached the centre of Istanbul, the sky was deep blue and shopkeepers were opening their shutters. Hakim placed the footrest and stool behind the taxi rank, and showed Ahmet where to stand. "This is my pitch. At first, you'll work with me – learn what to do. Then you'll get your own place."

Spreading an old newspaper on the ground, Hakim started the lesson. "Arrange the brushes on the paper, next to the rags. It's important to keep everything tidy. Next, open some tins of polish."

Carefully, Ahmet placed the brushes and rags on top of the newspaper. There was a photo of the Galiati football team on the back page, and he ran his finger over the headline, wondering what it said.

"Get ready!" said Hakim as a *dolmush* drew into the taxi rank. Businessmen got out of the cab, straightening their jackets, and Hakim gave a piercing yell. "Wanna impress your boss? Let me clean your shoes! Wanna lady friend? All the women love a man with shiny boots! Come to Hakim, the best shoe polisher in Istanbul!"

A middle-aged man sat down on the stool, placed his foot on the mount and pulled up a trouser leg, revealing a black sock and dusty shoe. Unfolding a fresh morning paper, he started to read.

"Look, Hakim! That's where we live!" Ahmet exclaimed, pointing over the customer's shoulder to a picture of Sulukule. "And there's a picture of that man Grandfather likes, the one who speaks out for us."

"Get your finger off the man's paper!" ordered Hakim. "We've no time for news! Hand me the black polish." Ahmet obeyed, sneaking another look at the paper, proud to see Sulukule on the front.

Crouching over the shoe, Hakim rubbed polish into the leather with circular strokes, before picking up a brush. "You must buff up and down, firm but gentle. If the leather's a bit worn, leave that bit, otherwise the *efendi* will sting you for a new pair of shoes. Rich people are the worst!" He gave the customer's shoes a final swish.

A shrill voice rang out from a nearby kiosk. "Get today's *HÜRRIYET* – all the latest news!" When a man in a smart suit handed some change to the news vendor, Ahmet stared at him, willing him over to Hakim's stand. The man glanced at the headlines and looked around. Ahmet gave him a smile and the man grinned back and strolled across to Hakim's pitch. Pulling up his trouser leg, he turned to the front page of his newspaper, reading as Hakim bent over his high-laced boot.

"This is a busy time, Ahmet," Hakim explained. "Everyone's going to work. You get all sorts, bankers, office workers, policemen – you have to be polite and work hard. Be specially careful with policemen!"

Ahmet looked at Hakim admiringly. Although his brother was only nine, he sounded like a professor.

"Here, you try, Ahmet," said Hakim, handing over the brush. Ahmet cautiously worked polish into the seam of the shoe, where the upper was stitched to the sole. As he worked, he hummed a popular tune. Laughing, the customer looked up from his paper and joined in. "Nice voice!" the man said. "And you've done a great job, son!"

"It's my first day," Ahmet told him.

"In that case, buy yourself a kebab on me." The man pushed some coins into Ahmet's hand. Standing up, he folded his paper, his eyes resting on the photo of Sulukule. Frowning, he patted Ahmet's head. "It's terrible what they're planning to do to your community, to the *Romanlar*. Ripping the heart out of the city – bulldozing a thousand years of heritage – sheer vandalism! Shouldn't be allowed. Just to build houses for a load of rich people. Urban renewal they call it. I call it wanton destruction!"

"What's he on about?" whispered Ahmet.

"Dunno," Hakim replied. "Just nod and smile. You often get clients talking in big words. If you pretend to listen, they leave a good tip!"

Hakim was right. As he left, the man took a note from his wallet and pushed it into the money tin.

"Look, there's Sadri," Hakim said, pointing at a passing friend from Sulukule. Sadri was carrying a huge silver tray of tea and glasses towards the taxi rank. He served some people waiting for a cab, pouring the golden liquid into the glasses from a great height.

"Hey, Sadri, it's my first day at work," Ahmet called.

"Two teas on the house, then!" Sadri smiled. "Good luck, young man."

Ahmet sipped the sweet tea, watching people pass by on their way to work or to the bazaar. Every now and then someone from Sulukule walked by, stooped under a wooden tray of *similar*, or laden with buckets of flowers, calling out their wares and waving at the brothers.

Ahmet polished ten pairs of shoes under Hakim's watchful gaze. "Go easy with the tongue and laces," warned Hakim. "Watch out you don't get polish all over the clients' socks. The trick is to rub very lightly over the laced bit, so the customer thinks you're polishing, but really you're just working a clean piece of cloth over it. That way, you get rid of the dust without wasting polish."

Ahmet wanted to sit down. His arms felt heavy, and the polish stung his fingers. But he worked on. Hakim smiled sympathetically. "Once the rush is over, we'll have something to eat."

The sound of the muezzin echoed round the street.

Hakim sighed. "That's the best place to be, by the mosque. But you'll never get that pitch unless you're related to the big fish!"

Ahmet nodded. His family and neighbours were always complaining about the richer, more powerful families who lived in Sulukule. The big fish ran the gangs of shoe polishers and flower sellers who worked the city. They kept the best pitches for their own sons and daughters, leaving the side alleys for the poorer children.

Soon, the brothers were sitting on the grass near the waterfront, with two sesame seed rolls and a bottle of water. Hakim gently rubbed Ahmet's fingers with a clean cloth. "We all get blisters at first. Your skin'll harden up in a few days."

Ahmet ran his thumb over his fingers. The blisters throbbed like a heart beat. He thought of his father working far away in Sweden. He thought of his mother making baklava for his birthday.

"Shoeshine scum! *Çingeneler!*" jeered some schoolboys, swinging their satchels as they ran by. Hakim chased them off.

"Posh rich gits!" he screamed.

"Lazy swots!" shouted Ahmet. The boys swerved away out of sight. "I wonder what it's like to go to school."

Hakim frowned. "They have to sit inside all day, reading boring books and writing long essays. They get blisters too, from holding their pens too tight. And no one pays them. I feel sorry for them, they're like babies. Like tourist children!"

"What are tourist children?"

Hakim smiled. "Come on, I'll show you."

Picking up his foot-mount, he led the way along the busy pavements, stopping outside a huge building.

"Hotel Cennet," said Hakim. "For people who come to Istanbul on holiday, rich Turks, as well as visitors from other countries. They're called tourists. They have lots of money. I try to guess where they're from. Then, if I talk to them in their language, I get a good tip. Watch this!"

Some guests had just come out of the hotel and were walking down the marble steps. "French," hissed Hakim. "Smart clothes, hair clean and tidy, woman in very high heels. Look at the kids in their new sandals!"

Ahmet giggled. The woman's short purple hair was covered with shiny lacquer. The two little girls wore frilly pink dresses with white belts, their spotless socks gleaming in the sun.

Hakim approached the man. "Bonjour monsieur, je netwoiyer sulier."

The man smiled. "Ah, mon gosse, tu parles français? Va-s-y!" Lifting his linen trouser leg, he stuck out a tan shoe.

"What's he saying?" asked Ahmet, impressed at his brother's command of French. Hakim grinned.

"He wants his shoes cleaning! He's pleased I speak French. Bet he gives a big tip."

Hakim gave Ahmet a share of the coins the man threw into the tin. Ahmet watched the girls, both older than him, skip off behind their elegant parents. He thought of his young sisters with their flowers, returning home hoarse after calling out to customers all day. He thought of his mother in her worn sandals and faded headscarf, cooking and cleaning, sewing dresses to sell in town.

At lunchtime, Ahmet bought a bottle of juice and a kebab with his tips. Finding a gap between the fishermen on the bridge, the brothers watched the huge ferries sailing on the Bosphorus. From the deck of a yacht, a woman in shorts and a bikini top waved at them. Ahmet gaped at her bare legs and arms till Hakim slapped his head and told him not to look.

For the rest of the afternoon, the boys worked in the tree-lined *meydan*, polishing the shoes of wealthy pensioners sitting in the square. "Time for a break!" Hakim announced. "Let's go to the courtyard of *Sultanahmet Cami*, and watch the worshippers going into the mosque. Then we'll go home."

The beautiful white building sparkled in the late afternoon sun, and as Hakim led him to the inner courtyard, Ahmet gazed at the dome and shimmering minarets. He sat silently with his brother on a warm marble bench, looking upwards until his head spun.

A guide leading a group of tourists stopped next to the bench. "Out of town farmers up from the country," whispered Hakim. "Look at their old-fashioned shoes."

The guide started to speak in a deep, velvety voice. Entranced, Ahmet listened to every word. "The mosque is a typical example of Late Classical Ottoman architecture. Begun in the rule of Ahmet the First, it was completed in 1616, taking seven years to build. It is the only mosque in the world with six minarets. We are blessed to live in a country which has such ancient and magnificent cultural treasures."

The tourists murmured in appreciation and followed the guide round the corner. "*Ya*, Ahmet!" Hakim exclaimed. "Imagine that! The Sultan who built the mosque has the same name as you!"

This is my mosque, Ahmet thought. It's so old, so huge, so beautiful, it will last for ever.

Twilight fell over Istanbul. Pigeons swarmed back to minarets, music blared from cafés and pavement stalls. Hakim picked up the foot-mount and stool, and stood up. "Come on. Time to go."

"This has been the best day of my life," Ahmet told his brother. "I've earned some money. I've been to the big mosque. I've seen boats going to far-off places. I've met people from France." He could feel his life unfolding before him with endless possibilities.

"And there'll be a special meal when we get home," Hakim reminded him.

Ahmet imagined a blue cake, with seven candles stuck into the icing.

A horse and cart pulled up in front of them and Mustafa leaned from his seat, waving his hand. "Want a lift, lads?" he shouted. "I can take you to the outskirts of Sulukule." Gratefully, the boys clambered into the cart.

Ahmet dozed, his head resting on a sack of flour. Hakim woke him as they neared their turning, and, grabbing their tools, the boys climbed from the cart and began to walk home through the darkness.

Ahmet's hands throbbed. Pain hammered his stiff shoulders like a battering ram. His box weighed him down, bruising his thigh as he dragged his feet over the path. Before him ran groups of Sulukule girls, shouting and giggling.

Suddenly, the girls stopped, frozen with shock. The evening breeze blew Amina's hair across her face, her skinny hand flew to her mouth.

Ahmet's aching body turned to stone. The stars trembled in the sky. The moon paled. He thought he could hear a *muezzin* calling, but it was the wailing of women. He began running through Sulukule, back to his home.

He saw mounds of broken bricks and rubble. His street had gone. His house had gone. The twisting ancient walkways had been destroyed. The music and laughter had disappeared. Ghostly eddies of dust danced around him, stinging his eyes.

Parts of Sulukule had been razed to the ground. Like metal monsters, gleaming faintly in the moonlight, the bulldozers stood in front of the remaining houses.

The shoebox thudded to the ravaged ground. Ahmet sat on the earth and wept.

Glossary

Romanlar – Roma (Turkish)

ibrik – long handled coffee pot (Turkish)

Öğreneceksin oğlum! – you'll find out, my boy! (Turkish)

dolmush – shared taxi (Turkish)

simitler – sesame seed rolls (Turkish)

efendi – Sir term of respect (Turkish)

Çingeneler – Gypsies (Turkish)

Bonjour monsieur, je netwoiyer sulier - shall I clean your shoes, sir? (broken French)

Ah, mon gosse, tu parles français? Va-s-y – Oh, my boy, you speak French? Okay (French)

meydan – a square (Turkish)

Sultanahmet Cami – mosque in centre of Istanbul (Turkish)

The Amazing Summer School for Gypsy Wannabees.

She was falling, falling. A thud. Darkness. Nothingness.

Voices.

"Was ist den loss?" "Qu'est qu'elle a fait?" "What the heck?"

Pain forced her eyes open. She couldn't breathe. Something bitter was oozing from her mouth. She closed her eyes again.

"Peri! Wake up!" someone screamed. "What happened?"

Peri couldn't move. She couldn't speak. Thoughts rushed across her mind like speeded up clouds in a film.

What happened is that I believed the glossy website with its bright images and clever graphics. I wanted to learn more Gypsy dances and more Romani. I so wanted it all to be true. And now I'm lying at the bottom of the stairs in a mansion in the hills of Serbia. I sensed there was something suss about this holiday, right from the start. From when Erik met me at Belgrade Airport.

"We meet all participants for Great Serbian Romani Summer School at airport!" Erik's grinning face had promised, looming from the Web. That, at least, had been true. At Belgrade Airport, Erik, the school director, had emerged from the waiting crowd, friendly, balding, brown-eyed.

Grabbing Peri's bags, Erik had rushed off to the car park. "This is Rosemary," he called over his shoulder, pointing to a woman holding a tuba case. Peri had noticed her at the Heathrow check-in, but lost sight of her as they boarded the plane. It's true, she thought, smiling at the large, pear-shaped lady. People end up looking like the instruments they play.

Unlocking the boot of a battered Mercedes, Erik placed the cases and the tuba inside, and eased himself into the driving seat. "Please to sit in back," he smiled. Peri squeezed in next to Rosemary, and Erik turned on the air conditioning and the radio. Soon they had left the city, and were driving through countryside.

Rosemary shouted over the blaring Balkan music. "Erik's amazing. You'll really like him. I was here last year. I enjoyed the course so much I simply had to come again. I've been playing tuba since secondary school, you see, but in Worthing, where I'm from, not many people are into the music I like."

Peri huddled in the folds of her coat, chilled by the freezing blasts from the air vents. She wanted to sleep, but Rosemary carried on talking. "I love Gypsy music!" she gushed. "It's so free, so full of passion and romance! Don't you agree? Is that why you came on this course, Peri?"

They were driving across a narrow bridge flanked by forested slopes. A river tumbled beneath them.

Why *have* I come, Peri thought, gazing out of the window. A great loss. A need to reconnect. A yearning since Nan's funeral. Recognising my own face in the crowd of mourners. Hearing snatches of *Romani* I couldn't quite understand.

"My grandmother was a Gypsy," she answered. "She married a non-Gypsy, never talked much about her heritage, but there were things she did that intrigued me. The way she'd never put her handbag on the ground. Never looked at people while they were eating. Stuff like that. Anyway, she left me £500 in her will, so I decided to spend it on this Gypsy Summer School before I start my new job. It's a kind of tribute to her..."

Rosemary was asleep. Peri dozed too, only waking when Erik slowed the car and blasted his horn. "We have come!" he announced. "We arrived at the Great Amazing Serbian Romani Summer School."

A bright star gleamed in the twilight. A good sign, thought Peri. Rosemary stretched and waved to the woman at the gates of the villa. "There's Auntie Manka. She hasn't changed a bit!"

Auntie Manka embraced Rosemary, greeted Peri, and helped Erik unload the car. Young people were drinking beer and juice on the vine-trellised terrace, a scene Peri recognised from the web pictures. "This is going to be the best holiday ever!" she said. She felt a connection with this place, with this village where generations of Roma had lived.

Erik led Peri and Rosemary to the terrace, where a pretty dark-haired student offered them drinks. "Hi, I am Delphine from Lille, and zis is Martina from Austria." Staring at Peri, she asked, "You are Roma, non? You 'ave ze look!"

"Well, half Roma, from London. You?"

"I too, I am ze meex. My fazer, 'e was Manouche. My muzzer, she eez French. We are ze sisters, non?" She grasped Peri's hand, and overwhelmed by tiredness and a sense of kinship, Peri gripped Delphine's fingers.

A tall lady with long auburn hair came up. "Hi, I'm Jodi. Peri, you and me are roommates. I'm an aerialist from Adelaide. I work in a circus. I've come to learn Gypsy clarinet. What do you do?"

"I've just left College – studied dance and acting. I'm joining a *Romani* Dance Company next month, so I've come to learn more dancing and some *Romani* language. I used to speak a little, but I hardly use it now."

She smiled, remembering Nan teaching her words while they cooked together.

After an evening meal of white cheese, bread and pale green olives, Peri showered, unpacked and fell into bed.

Next morning she was woken by a tapping sound. Jodi was standing on her head whilst typing on a laptop. Squeezing past her roommate, Peri went to shower.

There were eight people at the breakfast table – five students, Zita the dance teacher, Auntie Manka and Erik. "Zita is professional wedding dancer," Erik told the guests, "and my Auntie Manka works the part-time job at a Roma cloth boutique in town. She also cooks and cleans for the Summer School. We take you to shop one day, you buy Gypsy cloths. Special price for students!"

"Yeah, twice the usual amount I reckon!" Jodi whispered.

"And this is Diki the dog," Erik said, pointing at a black and white spaniel hiding under the table.

Peri smoothed her linen napkin. On the table, a selection of white food gleamed in the morning light. Cream cheese, butter the colour of ivory, peeled leeks, hardboiled eggs, a jug of milk, and china bowls piled with groats.

Erik stood up and cleared his throat. "I shall like to welcome all to Great Serbian Romani Summer School!" he smiled, glancing at his watch. "I am school organiser, I also shall drive you somewhere you would need to go. I shall collect students from the airport, and I shall teach violin, cello, clarinet, singing, and *Romani* language."

"One man band!" Peri muttered.

Rosemary nodded. "Told you he's wonderful, didn't I!"

Zita stood up. "Peri and Martina, you are my dance students. Come, let's go." Gracefully leading the way to the terrace, Zita slotted a tape into a cassette recorder, and demonstrated a sequence of simple moves. "*Ek, dui, trin, shtar,*" she counted.

Peri followed her, but Martina couldn't get it. "*Ek, dui, trin, shtar,*" Zita repeated, demonstrating the steps in very slow motion. Martina went in the wrong direction. "*Ek, dui, trin, shtar,*" Zita chanted. Martina tripped up. Zita stood next to Martina, nodding at

Peri to stand the other side. *"Ek, dui, trin, shtar,"* they chorused. After half an hour, Martina managed to walk four steps forward and three back.

I've paid £500 to learn a dance I already know, Peri thought irritably as they broke for orange juice and biscuits. The words RIP-OFF flashed through her mind. Taking her drink to the back of the garden, she sat under a tree. When Diki wandered up, she shared a biscuit with him. "I hope things get better," she mumbled. "Zita's a great dancer, but she's not a great teacher. I wonder if she's ever taught before. This is a long way to come for a scam."

Diki laid his head on her knee in sympathy and Peri patted him and smiled. "Probably first day teething troubles."

It was late morning when Erik came to find her, explaining he wouldn't be giving her the scheduled *Romani* lesson that day. "I must to go to town to collect DVD," he said. "But don't worry, my grandmother has agreed to teach. Come. I show her house."

Disappointed, Peri followed Erik to the adjoining villa where an ancient woman in a blue flowered apron was shucking peas into a pot. Erik greeted his grandmother, who embraced Peri, gesturing her to sit down.

"Grandma shall tell story in *Romani* language," Erik said. "Write down what she is saying, and this evening you read at me. Then we translate. Is great way to learning language."

Jingling his car keys, Erik left the house, whistling a tune. Peri stared at Grandma. Talking rapidly, the old woman filled a long-handled pot with water and brewed coffee. Peri didn't understand what she was saying. The language was nothing like the *Romani* Nan used to speak. Perhaps the woman was talking in Serbian.

Grandma handed Peri a cup of fragrant coffee and sat down. There was a long silence. "Do you speak English?" Peri asked. There was no response. Grandma continued to wait calmly, taking little sips of coffee. Peri tried again. "Sprechen Sie Deutsch? Parlez-vous français?"

Grandma began to talk, words tumbling out of her mouth in an incomprehensible torrent. This is ridiculous, thought Peri. Crazy way to learn a language.

Grandma started sobbing, her tears dripping onto Peri's notebook. Alarmed, Peri patted the old woman's bony hand. Grandma began to talk more slowly. *"Manka,"* wept Grandma, gesticulating to Peri to write. Obediently Peri wrote, '*Manka.*' From another rush of words, Peri recognised the name *Erik*. Staring at the names, Peri guessed that Grandma was using this lesson to convey her feelings to her relations.

40

Grandma continued, insisting Peri write down every word. "I feel like a secretary with a mad boss," Peri groaned, clutching her pen. Her hand ached, but still the old lady talked, tapping her fingers impatiently whenever Peri stopped scribbling.

A shrill clanging interrupted the lesson. Auntie Manka was leaning over the dividing garden wall, ringing a bell. Grandma made eating gestures and pushed Peri out of the door. Diki was waiting outside, and jumped up to lick Peri's hand. "This is getting more bizarre by the minute!" Peri told the dog. "I've got a mad roommate, a hopeless dance teacher and now I've been saddled with a crazy old woman."

Lunch was another white meal with bread, chicken, halumi, pale tomatoes, peeled apples, and yoghurt soup.

"White food is really good for the lymph glands," Rosemary explained. "How was your lesson?"

"Unusual," Peri replied diplomatically. "Yours?"

Rosemary grabbed a handful of cheese. "Great! A Gypsy from the village came up to teach me. We're learning *Jovano, Jovanke*. I really feel I'm getting to grips with *Romani* music at last."

Jodi prodded the tomatoes suspiciously with her fork. "*Jovano, Jovanke*, that's not a *Romani* song, it's Macedonian!"

Rosemary scowled. "No it isn't! The teacher said it was a Gypsy song. You can tell it's *Romani*, it sounds like all the rest of their music. That's right, isn't it, Peri?"

Pretending not to hear, Peri offered round the cheese.

Martina sliced off a piece of chicken and speared it with her fork. "So vonderful a dance lesson, was it not?" she grinned at Peri. "I cannot wait for the next."

Despite the heat of the afternoon, it was cool on the shady terrace. Zita demonstrated the steps she'd shown that morning. Bored, Peri began to think of her brothers and sisters back home. *Wonder what Dave's doing, and Mimi and Zak. I wish Ma had taken Nan's inheritance like I wanted, instead of encouraging me to come on this course.*

After the lesson she found Jodi in the bedroom, tapping away on her laptop again. Peri lay on her bed and studied the words she'd written down that morning. Apart from *Manka* and *Erik*, nothing made much sense.

Erik knocked on the door. "I look dictation now," he announced, taking Peri to the dining room where Auntie Manka and Zita were laying the table. Erik pointed to a large sofa and Peri sank into the lumpy cushions.

"So," said Erik, putting on his glasses. "What Grandmother teach?"

"Not much, to be honest. I don't think I'm going to get very far with her. Don't you have a *Romani* text book? I'd rather read some stories and practice speaking."

"No, no! This is most best way. Say me what she say you."

Peri read out the garbled words. Auntie Manka coughed in embarrassment and Erik grinned. So my hunch *was* right, Peri thought. Grandma's using me as a secret weapon to tell her relatives what she thinks of them.

Erik leaned forward and squinted at the scribble. "Okay, now I translate you some words."

"Erik, I really need structured lessons..." Peri objected.

"No, you will use to it. All students learning like this."

The week was almost over. "*Ek, dui, trin, shtar,*" in the mornings, repeating the same steps over and over. Grandma's rambling stories washed down with coffee before lunch. Erik's amused translations in the afternoon. The constant theme tune of *Jovano, Jovanke* played on various instruments, floating down the stairs from the rehearsal room.

"I've never been so fed-up in my life!" Peri complained to her roommate. "I thought it would be exciting, learning *Romani*, dancing in the heartland of Gypsy culture. But I'm not learning anything, and I'm bored."

"Haven't you heard?" Jodi asked. "Erik's taking us all on a trip this avo. That'll brighten things up."

"Great! It'll be good to have a look round town and buy some souvenirs!"

Erik assembled the students after lunch. "We shall go on outing. To cemetery for grave feast. Today is anniversary of Grandfather's death."

A cold shiver went down Peri's spine as they drove out of the village. At the graveyard, she followed Erik through the long grass and wild flowers, trying not to look at the rows of marble headstones.

Grandma, wearing a new scarf, lamented loudly, beating her chest, while Auntie Manka swept the white tomb with a soft broom, chanting prayers. When the area was clean, a cloth was spread over the tomb, and bottles of Vimto and packets of biscuits were laid out.

As Auntie Manka lit candles and incense, a tongue of fire shot up into the air, making everyone gasp. An enormous church candle, housed in an urn, had burst into flames, spitting sparks at Peri.

"How spooky is that!" Peri shuddered, as a black shadow passed over her.

"It is a vampire," screeched Martina. "Dracula!"

"But eez ze wrong country," Delphine corrected. "This is Serbie, not Ungari. Dracula is Ungari, non?"

As soon as they got back to the School, Peri went to the bathroom to shower away the dust and smell of death. She shampooed her hair, shaking it back, enjoying its damp weight on her skin. "I look like Nan," she said to her blurred reflection in the mirror. "Same green eyes, same curly hair and olive skin."

Dressed in clean jeans and blouse, she started downstairs.

And then she was falling, falling into a black pit, into a nothingness, twisting and turning. She heard a sickening thud.

She was woken by the twittering of birds. "Was ist den loss?" "Qu'est qu'elle a fait?" "What the heck?"

Cautiously opening her eyes, she saw feet. Some bare. Some in socks. A red stain on the carpet. Blood.

Who is this person, this corpse? she wondered. Why does my chest hurt so much? A piercing laugh jangled round the corridor, a note so high it was off the tonal scale.

"Elle est hystérique!" commented Delphine, trying to pull Peri to her feet. But Peri couldn't move. She was carried into the bedroom. When she opened her eyes again, two hands were floating above her, and the laughter grew louder.

"It's okay, doll, I'm only doing Reiki," explained Jodi.

"I know also ze Reiki," said Martina excitedly, and suddenly four hands floated in the air. Peri sank back into darkness.

A shadow loomed above her. Erik was standing over her, brandishing a small bottle and some cotton wool. "You cut lip when you fall. It is very big!" he said, smearing something round Peri's mouth.

Pain seared her gums and she jerked away, tears spilling down her cheeks. She tasted blood. Her mouth was swelling rapidly where a tooth had sliced into her lip.

"You must call a doctor!" said Jodi. "Get her a doctor! She fell really heavily. I heard her crash down the stairs. She's probably broken her ribs."

"No, she is okay." Erik answered confidently. "Not need for bothering doctor. Grandma has ointments for everything."

Grandma was sent off to bring medication, returning with some linctus that smelt of fried sausages. The students were ushered out while the ointment was poured onto a clean rag and applied to Peri's ribs.

Peri fell asleep, dreaming of greasy burgers and onions at Appleby Fair.

The next day was a haze of agony and pain, accompanied by the squeaky echo of *Jovano, Jovanke*. Jodi brought trays of white food at breakfast time and lunch, and Grandma arrived every few hours to spread more vile-smelling liquid on the bruises. Peri's lip had swollen so much she couldn't speak. Every time she moved, a burning pain shot through her chest.

"I'm not having this!" Jodi announced. "I'm going to get that *gallah* to change your flight and send you home. You should be in hospital, I reckon!"

The next day, Peri was led into the garden, where the other students had gathered to wave her off.

In her honour, they'd dressed in the bright scarves and swirling red polka dot skirts they'd bought from Auntie Manka's Gypsy boutique the previous evening. But they didn't look like *Romani* women. Martina looked like an Austrian peasant, Rosemary like an overweight bank clerk. Square shouldered Jodi resembled a weight-lifter, and Delphine looked like a chorus girl from *Les Miserables*. Only Zita, in her tight jeans and fitted blouse, looked like a Gypsy.

"Gypsy wannabees!" Peri mumbled painfully to Erik as they drove to the airport. "You're running a school for Gypsy wannabees." Erik smiled and slotted a disc into the deck.

The sound of *Jovano, Jovanke* filled the Mercedes.

Glossary

Was ist den loss? – What's up? (German)

Qu'est qu'elle a fait? – What's she done? (French)

Ek, dui, trin, shtar – one, two, three, four (*Romani*)

Jovano, Jovanke – A well-known Macedonian folk song [Rosemary mistakenly assumes it to be *Romani* song]

Elle est hystérique – she's hysterical (French)

gallah – name of bird – used as term of abuse in Australia

The Boy who wouldn't Speak

Ferdi hunched over the desk, studying the worksheet.

Gina glanced at the notes sent through by the Head of Music Therapy. Ferdinand Krasniqi, nine years old, born in Kosovo just before the break up of Yugoslavia, moved to Germany at the age of five, came to England six months ago. Stopped talking one week after arrival.

The child placed his pen on the desk, tucking up the sleeves of his shirt. "Finished?" Gina asked. He nodded and she handed him a box with different shaped holes cut in the sides. Ferdi looked at the box, turning it round in his slim hands. He glanced at Gina as if asking what he was supposed to do.

Gina picked up a handful of wooden cut-outs. "See these bits of wood? It's like a jigsaw puzzle – you have to slip each shape through the right slot." The last child she'd seen had taken some time to work out which shape fitted through the correct hole, but Ferdi immediately inserted the shapes into the box, his brown eyes gleaming when a piece landed inside the container.

No problem there, Gina thought. He understands my instructions and he's extremely dextrous and well coordinated.

Taking out the vocabulary test cards, she wriggled into a small chair next to the boy and laid pictures of food on the desk. "What's your favourite food, Ferdi?" she asked. "I like apples best. What do you like?"

Ferdi pointed to an orange.

"Can you say orange for me?"

Ferdi drew an orange on his worksheet. When the buzzer signalled the end of the session, Ferdi looked up, then continued colouring his picture.

Gina stood up. "Right. Let's go and find your mum and arrange another appointment."

She opened the door to the waiting room and Ferdi ran over to his mother. "Your son did really well, Mrs. Krasniqi," Gina said. "I'd like a bit more information from you about language usage, if you don't mind."

She flipped her notepad open. "What language do you speak at home?"

Ferdi's mother smoothed down her long black skirt. "Romanes, the Gypsy language."

"And what other languages has your son been exposed to?"

"Exposed to?" The woman looked alarmed.

Gina grinned. "Sorry! Standard textbook query. It sounds like I'm talking about infectious illnesses, doesn't it? I just need to know what other languages you speak."

"Well, in Kosovo, we spoke Albanian and Serbian, then we learnt German in Berlin, and now of course, English," the woman answered. "I learnt English at College in my country, so it is quite easy for me, but my husband finds it difficult."

"Mother – fluent English with slight accent," Gina scribbled on her pad as Mrs. Krasniqi continued.

"My other children talk Romanes to their father and me, Albanian or Serbian with friends from our country, German to each other, and English at school. It is only Ferdi who cannot talk."

Mrs. Krasniqi fingered the edge of her blouse, rubbing at the bright material. "Sometimes I wonder if it is because of the war, because of what he has seen. Neighbours turning on each other, former friends shouting abuse. Killings." Her voice broke, and she took a deep breath. "But my other children have seen the same things, and they all speak. Why is Ferdi like this?"

Gina looked at the file again. The notes showed there was nothing medically wrong with the child. The speech therapist had confirmed that Ferdi's teeth and jaw were in alignment, he had no hearing problems, and his vocal chords were undamaged. The social worker reported that the boy was in good health, and came from a loving family, with no history of abuse.

So why wouldn't Ferdi talk?

"I'm sure I can help your son," Gina assured Mrs. Krasniqi. "I'd like to see him again in a few days. The receptionist will make an appointment for you."

She kept a bowl of lollipops on the table. "You've done really well, Ferdi," Gina said. "Take a lollipop to eat on the way home." With a slight bow, the boy chose a red one, passing it to his mother. Mrs. Krasniqi held Ferdi's hand, turning as they reached the door. "Madame, my son is a good, kind boy. He gives me this lollipop so I can give to his little brother. This is the sort of child he is. Please, madame, help him to talk."

As Gina tidied up the consulting room, she remembered her own childhood confusion over language. She'd been humiliated one birthday when her grandfather complained about her poor Turkish. "Çok güzel," he mocked in a Cockney accent. "You sound like a London girl!"

"It's not my fault!" Gina had shouted. "I *am* a London girl. It's because of you we're all here. Don't blame me because you haven't taught me your language! I speak English!" She'd got a smack for that!

It was language conflict that had influenced her decision to become a music therapist. She was drawn to the concept that music was a zone between words and thoughts, an art form that helped clients reveal feelings they couldn't otherwise express. Music and movement unlocked the secrets of the soul and helped the mute to speak.

Her University thesis, *Music; A Cure for Language Loss,* dealt with the harmful effect multilingualism could have on children's speech development. Research showed that more bilingual kids developed a stutter than monolingual ones. Sometimes the stutter occurred in the dominant language, thought to be caused by syntactic overload. Cognitive overload made some children switch languages in mid-sentence. She herself had done this as a child, beginning a sentence in Turkish, then changing to English and finishing off in Kurdish. That was okay at home, but when she did this at school, her friends laughed and the teachers didn't know what she meant.

By the time she was nine, she'd begun to stammer so badly she'd been sent to a speech therapist. But the speech therapist had focussed on mechanical actions, giving Gina exercises to isolate the tongue and palette, making her practice word combinations which made the stutter even worse.

That's when she'd stopped talking, seeking refuge in silence. That way she didn't have to choose which language to speak. It was too complicated. Her mother spoke Kurdish, her father Turkish, and at school she had to talk English. Sometimes, fearful of causing anger or derision, she didn't know which language to use.

In the world of silence, she was free.

One day, in the music lesson, when Mr. Barlowe was ill, the supply teacher had unexpectedly asked Gina to sing a solo, and to everyone's surprise, she'd sung loudly, the lyrics flowing from her mouth. Gina was surprised too. This is magic, she thought. Maybe if I sing what I want to say, the words will come out more easily. So she developed the habit of singing her thoughts very quietly to herself before saying them out loud. And gradually the stammer faded away.

She glanced at the notes again, seeing that in Kosovo, Ferdi's father had been a journalist, his mother a teacher. In England, Mr. Krasniqi was a taxi driver, and Mrs. Krasniqi was unemployed. The child had lived in different countries, surrounded by different customs and sounds. It was highly possible that his life, full of sudden ruptures and changes, had caused a classic case of elective mutism. Hearing so many languages had overloaded his brain, leading to confusion and anxiety. Gina believed Ferdi simply didn't know which language was appropriate to use, and he therefore used none.

At University she'd read a case study about an immigrant whose family had moved from Hong Kong to Scotland. Years later, remembering his difficulties at school, the man wrote a poem about his experience:

I speak with two voices
but one is quieter than the other.
There are two mouths in my face,
but one is bigger than the other.
Two tongues dribbling
two scripts scribbling.
I talk in chords
of misunderstanding.

The poem echoed in Gina's head as she drove home. The lines pounded in her brain as she queued at the supermarket and in the kitchen as she prepared a meal. The words haunted her as her partner poured her a glass of wine and told her about the latest stock market crisis.

Before Ferdi's next visit, Gina placed a selection of musical instruments round the consulting room. When Ferdi came in, his eyes lit up and he walked straight over to the yellow xylophone. He banged the metal slats, picking out a tune that Gina recognised from her childhood. She called Mrs. Krasniqi from the waiting area, and a smile spread over the woman's anxious face as Ferdi played the melody.

"What is that tune?" Gina asked.

"It is a Turkish song we Roma in Kosovo sing," said Mrs. Krasniqi, tapping her foot. Ferdi began to play louder, and unable to resist the catchy tune, Mrs. Krasniqi began to dance. Gina found herself standing up too, moving her hips to the rhythm. How unprofessional! she thought, captivated by the music. Ferdi laughed at the dancing women, thumping the yellow slats harder.

And then Gina heard a buzz, like the drone of a bee. Ferdi was humming. He stopped and cleared his throat.

"This is a real breakthrough," Gina whispered to Mrs. Krasniqi. "Your son has made a sound. He used his vocal chords." Ferdi carried on playing, and the women took up the melody, smiling as they moved around the room. Gina grabbed a tambourine while Mrs. Krasniqi swished her long skirt from side to side. Ferdi put down the xylophone sticks and jumped up, dancing with his mother, shaking his shoulders and snapping his fingers.

And he began to sing.

Glossary

çok güzel – very nice   (Turkish)

La Dolce Vita

From the archives of BritRom Tribune:

In June 2008, journalist Mary O'Connor went to Italy for our magazine to interview 16 year old Gabi, a Roma girl originally from a village just outside Bucharest. Here is Mary's report.

Gabi is a small, pretty teenager, with long black hair and dark eyes. Dressed in jeans and a yellow T-shirt, her golden earrings swing as she talks about her life and why her family left their birthplace.

"It was horrible being a Roma in Romania," Gabi tells me in fluent Italian. "We lived in awful conditions, in shacks without water or electricity. As if we didn't deserve the amenities that everyone else takes for granted. Romania is a poor land, and some of our countrymen and women live without running water and electricity. But most non-Roma have access to wells and rivers, whilst *we* have open sewers running through our villages."

I ask if she can describe the atmosphere when Romania finally joined the EEC in 2004.

Gabi grins. "Of course. It was a wonderful time. We felt as if the door of a prison had been thrown open. I was twelve. All us Roma, we dreamed of moving to Western Europe, finding work, getting a good education. Living a decent life. It's normal. People always move to other countries to improve their fate. Actually, my mum didn't want to leave Romania. She wanted to stay in our beautiful country, she said the hills and forests had sheltered her parents during the war. You know, when the Nazis ..."

She sighs. "But my father didn't want life to continue in the same old way. At last Mama agreed it was better to go abroad, somewhere where my dad could find employment."

A child wanders up to look at my tiny recording device. She reaches out her sticky fingers, but Gabi takes the girl in her arms. "Florina, my little sister," she says.

"What made your parents choose Italy?"

"It's not so far from Romania. And people say Italian is like Romanian. Actually, we found it's not really so like Romanian, but lots of words are similar so even when we first arrived we could understand a little. My dad arranged to stay with some relatives. When we arrived at Rome airport, he phoned the number they'd given him. A stranger answered. He said our family had left some weeks before. We started crying, and wandered round the airport and saw a Rom with an accordion. We asked him where we could go. And he told us about this area under the bridge. It was near the airport, so we just picked up our cases and walked."

At this point Gabi's eyes fill with tears. "Do you think we want to live like this?" she asks, pointing to the tent in the narrow gully she now calls home. "We left a land where at least we had an old house, where we had friends and family, to come to another country where we are despised, where people want to murder us. Italian spit is the same as Romanian spit! When the rats come out at night, my brother asks Mama why we don't go home. Then Mama reminds us that it was even worse in Romania. Here Papa can find good work, and as we have papers, we are allowed to go to school."

Romica, Gabi's mother, bustles out of the tent. The hem of her long flowered dress skims the mud as she brings me a cup of coffee.

"Mama, I told the journalist that you say it was worse for us in Romania," says Gabi.

Romica adjusts the scarf knotted round her head. Her Italian is not very good, but I manage to understand her. "That's right, otherwise why else would we stay here? When we first came it wasn't so bad – my husband found work and the kids went to school. But now things are changing for the Roma. Many Italians hate us. Only last week, Roma huts were burnt in Naples, and the authorities want to fingerprint us. They accuse us of every theft, of every assault – but I want to ask one question. Who was it who invented the Mafia? Was it us, the Roma, or was it the Italians themselves?"

Romica's eyes glitter angrily and she crosses herself and mutters a prayer. "I know that a poor teacher was beaten to death by a Romanian, it was a terrible crime. But are all the murders in Italy only committed by Romanians? And are all people from Romania Gypsies? They blame us for everything, they accuse us of kidnapping Italian children. That's a joke! Haven't we enough children to feed without taking theirs?"

"Papa!" Florina cries, wriggling from Gabi's arms. A thin man is trudging up the path towards us, a heavy cloth bag slung over his shoulder. He waves, his face lined with exhaustion, picks up Florina and kisses her.

"Zoltan," the man introduces himself, lowering himself onto the tarpaulin sheet on the ground. I ask him why he stays in Rome, now the situation for Gypsies is worsening.

"He can't speak Italian," Gabi explains. "I'll translate for you."

She talks quickly to her father in *Romani*, and he shrugs and replies. "Here I can earn ten times more than I earned back home. There I often couldn't find work – many people won't employ Gypsies. When we *do* find work in Romania, it's cleaning sewers, shifting manure. No one will consider us for a good job with a decent salary and prospects. There, my uncle and aunt were murdered by skinheads – a gang came from town and firebombed their house. Here I work as a house painter – I get a good wage, even on the black market, and it's a peaceful steady job. All I want is for my children to get an education and live in a decent home."

Zoltan shakes his head, and I glimpse a drop of water on his cheek. Sweat or tears, I wonder. He speaks in a low voice, and waits for his daughter to translate. "My friend wasn't at work today. Did you hear about the girls who drowned? One of the girls was his niece, his sister's daughter. They say the holidaymakers went on sunbathing, while the bodies of our children lay on the beach. At least someone covered them with towels. That person will go to heaven. We came here to escape racism, but the way things are going, we live in fear. There is nowhere for us to go. We thought that in Western Europe, there would be a place for us. Sometimes I feel like..."

He stares bleakly at the wall. He says something to Gabi and she runs into the tent, coming back with a cup of coffee for her father and an exercise book which she hands to me. "My English homework," she says.

"Do you enjoy school?" I ask her.

"I enjoy it, but some pupils say horrible things about Gypsies. They say we *deserve* to be burnt, that we should all go home. It makes me scared and sad. I am always worried they will beat up my little sister. And my young brother is so frightened he won't go to school anyway."

Her homework is to write an essay in English about her neighbourhood. She asks me to correct the errors in her neatly written text.

My house is in Rome. Rome is the capital of Italy. We have a big house, with one bedroom of every person. My mother and my father have a very big room with a enormous televisione and a piano. Our bath is very big. In the kichen we have a electric cooker. Our garden is very beautiful. We have much flowers, red roses and my father grow vejtables.

I correct her mistakes and smile, feeling something trickle down my own cheek.

Sweat or tears?

Toffee Apple King

Tim closed the latest report from the Office of Fair Trading, pushed back his chair and looked down at the river.

The Millenium Dome glimmered in the late morning sun and a gull flew past, making for the mudflats of Greenwich.

As the bird winged away, Tim felt a sense of futility and frustration. "What am I doing here?" he asked himself. "I'm supposed to be finding ways of minimising company losses, but we should be paying twice as much tax as we are!"

The intercom buzzed and Charles' voice blasted through the office. "Hey, Tim. Ready to lunch?"

Tim shrugged on his grey jacket. "On my way," he replied.

Emma and Sujata were chatting in the lift bay.

"O, hello Tim!" said Emma. "I'm just telling Suj I'm off to The Maldives next week. Can't wait. Fresh air, blue sky, warm sea!"

"Lucky cow!" Sujata said.

"Hey, you've just had a week in Dubai!" Emma reminded her as the lift arrived.

"Any holiday plans, Tim?" Sujata asked.

"No, I'll take a break towards the end of the year." Tim pushed into the lift behind his colleagues, squeezing next to Hassan and James from Equities. Loosening his tie, he nodded at the two men as the elevator hurtled downwards.

Charles met them on the ground floor. "What kept you?" he asked. Without waiting for an answer, he strode to the exit, shouting, "Come on! Keep up! You are all so slow – time is money!" Sujata smiled at Tim as they walked to Wagamamas. The wind funnelled through the tall buildings of Canary Wharf, whipping Tim's chestnut hair across his face. He stopped for a moment, watching a plastic bag sail up into the sky.

Wagamamas was crowded with the usual customers in designer clothes, all talking about the grim economic situation. Emma picked up a newspaper from the table, flicking through while she sipped a carrot juice.

"ILLEGAL SITE THREATENS GREEN BELT PEACE," she read out.

Charles almost choked on his sushi. "Don't know why the government doesn't do something about those blasted Gypsies!" he fumed. "Dirty thieving lot. We've got some trying to camp outside our village, so we've started an Action Committee. It's a health hazard, the way they live. And the thought of their scabby kids being in the same class as my Giles......"

His voice tailed off in horror.

"The Press always exaggerate," Sujata objected. "Remember that STAMP ON THE CAMPS rubbish the Sun ran some years ago? Gypsies can't be as dirty and diseased as the bigots claim, otherwise they'd have died off centuries ago."

Charles slammed down his glass. "O, you're just prejudiced, because their ancestors came from India!"

Everyone laughed except Tim. He clenched his hands, trying to control his anger. This was the moment he'd been dreading, the moment his parents had warned him about when he got into University.

"Soon as they know you're a Traveller, you'll be teased and bullied," Dad had warned. "What do you want a degree for? Haven't me and your Ma done well enough with no book learning? You can read and write, what more do you need?"

Tim hadn't listened. He'd always found studying easy, coming top of his class. "I won't tell anyone I'm a Traveller," he'd replied. "I'll say I'm French if anyone says I look foreign! And a Degree in Business will help us all."

"No good'll come of denying your heritage, son, you mark my words. You should be proud of who you are. Work with your own kind! There's a good job waiting for you on the stall." Then Dad repeated the claim Tim had heard throughout his childhood. "Our family introduced toffee apples into England five hundred years ago – one of our ancestors was called the Toffee Apple King. Now that's something to be proud of."

"I *am* proud of it, Dad, but I still wanna study!"

So Tim had gone to University – president of the Debating Society, winner of the Chess Tournament two years in a row, member of the Equestrian Club – and left with a first class degree in Business Studies.

The STAMP ON THE CAMPS slogan hammered in his head.

"What do you think, Tim?" Charles appealed for support. "You wouldn't want a load of wasters at the end of your road, would you? Messing up the lovely home you've worked for! Leaving rubbish and filth all over the place."

Tim gripped the edge of the table, restraining himself from landing a punch on Charles' smug pink face. I've got to get away from this life, he thought. Before I'm completely tainted by greed and self-interest.

He stood up, ripping off his tie.

"I'm not doing this any more!" he announced. "You can stick your sushi and your suits and your bonuses."

The others stared at him in astonishment. "Sit down, Tim," Sujata said. "Have some jasmine tea."

Tim screwed up his tie. "I'm one of the dirty rabble Charles has been ranting about. I'm a Gypsy."

Charles cackled like a goose. "O yah, right! And I'm a bus driver! Come on, Tim, stop talking rubbish. Sit down, finish your meal. You've been overworking."

Emma stared at Tim, then at Charles. Sujata poked her noodles with her chopsticks.

Tim felt himself growing taller, towering above the diners. He glared down at Charles. "You think you're better than people who live in trailers," he said quietly. "Well, I was born on a Traveller site. And that makes me better than you! It gives me an edge. Do you know what it's like to be followed home from school, have kids throw stones and call you names? Do you know what it's like when no one will sit next to you in class, because they say you're dirty. Well, I do! And the fact I survived makes me an excellent businessman!"

Customers were looking over at their table.

"Tim, sit down, your *miso ramen*'s getting cold," Emma urged.

"Stuff the *miso ramen*! I'm going!"

As he reached the door, he turned round. For the first time in years he felt free. An idea came to him, and waving his tie like a flag, he announced, "Shove your corporate business and your gold plated pensions. I'm off to sell toffee apples."

⁘⫷✶⫸⁘

A white truck with the words KING OF THE TOFFEE APPLES on its side stood in a field at Stow Fair. Inside the van, a smiling woman speared an apple onto a stick, passing it to an assistant who swirled the apple in a thick sticky liquid. The apple was plunged into a vat of cold water, and placed on a square of red cellophane. At the counter, a man with a silver earring deftly twisted the cellophane round the apple, handing it over to the little girl at the front of the queue.

The three workers joked and called good-natured insults to each other and the waiting crowd. Wasps buzzed round the vat, the smell of melted sugar sweetened the air.

"Hello, Tim! Two please."

Tim almost dropped the apple he was holding. "Suj! How did you know where I'd be?"

"I didn't," Sujata laughed. "Suresh was hungry and ran over to your van." She unwrapped the apple and passed it to the small boy by her side.

"Who's the boy? Is he yours? What are you doing here?"

"My aunt's family lives in Cheltenham – I've come down for the weekend. They always come to the Fair – they say it reminds them of Delhi. Suresh is my nephew."

"Top toffee apple," Suresh grinned.

"On the house!" said Tim, waving away Sujata's coins. Pushing her heavy hair behind her shoulders, Sujata smiled her thanks.

"You seem so different," Tim told her. "It's the first time I've seen you in jeans and with your hair like that. You look ten years younger. Tell you what! Can you meet me in Sitara on Engel Street about seven? We can catch up over a meal. I can get away early if these two'll clear up. Meet Danny and Janie, my brother and sister."

"We do all the work around here!" Janie said. "The lad's grown soft after living in London! Dad always said he'd be back, knew he wouldn't be able to keep away."

"Couldn't hack his posh job, more like!" jeered Danny.

That evening, Tim waited for Sujata in the restaurant, drumming his fingers in time to the piped music. She won't come, he thought. Why would a high flyer like her want to bother with someone like me? In her world I'm a dropout, a loser.

The candle on his table flickered as the outer door opened. It won't be her, Tim thought, staring at the picture on the wall.

"Sorry I'm late, Tim," Sujata apologised. "Some unexpected guests turned up and I had to help my auntie cook."

She stood before him, beautiful in a maroon dress. Her smile lit up the room. The waiter rushed to take her jacket and she sat down, unfolding her napkin. Tim wanted to tell her how lovely she looked, but the words stuck in his throat. "How's it been at work?" he asked.

"Same as usual," Sujata replied, as the waiter brought popadum and pickles to the table. "You really upset the applecart when you left – the MD tried to find you and ask you to come back. Wanted to offer a promotion, so his PA said. Said it would be good for the company profile to build some Ethnic Minority Projects. Apparently he wanted to develop banking ideas with the Travelling community."

Tim laughed. "Why doesn't that surprise me? Shows how much he knows about Travellers! And as for promotion, more like keeping me in my place!"

"Tell me about it! I'm Asian and a woman, so he gets two points for me! But I'll stay in the corporate world for a bit, learn what I need. Then I'm going to work in the Voluntary Sector, VSO or something. Do something worthwhile."

The waiter returned with thalis of rice and vegetables. Breaking off a piece of naan, Sujata scooped up some korma. "Don't you find this all a bit low key?" she asked. "I mean, selling at fairs after the world of high finance?"

Tim heaped rice on his plate, spooning on sag aloo and chicken. "You're sending me up, right? All my studies and work experience have led to this. Think about it! Canary Wharf is like a fairground without the fun. I still do marketing, buying the best produce as cheaply as possible, finding outlets, fostering customer relationships, doing market research and so on."

He sipped his beer. "According to my Dad, it's in the blood. Our family's been in toffee apples for centuries, introduced them into England, so the old man reckons. He's not too well, so I'm happy to work with my folks, expand the business. Dad's always used old-fashioned methods, like handshakes and memory, so we've started computerising the databases. It's a real challenge to drag the business into the twenty first century!"

Sujata lay down her napkin. "I hear what you're saying, but I'm not convinced. I spent last week at a meeting in Brussels, and I'm off to New York next month for work. Don't you miss the travelling?"

Tim stared at the candle flame. "I've got other connections now, more meaningful. We're selling toffee apples at a Roma event in Stockholm soon, and making links with international Traveller organisations. And now it's summer, there's nothing like it, Suj – out in the fresh air, meeting kids, having a laugh with their parents, with the traders, turning up at Fairs with other Gypsies and Travellers. It's not quite G8 or Davos, but it's real and it's fun!"

He loosened a button on his shirt. "Every time I remember the office, the tinted double glazed windows that don't open, the pointless hierarchy, snooty executives like Charles, I know I made the right decision. For the first time in years I feel fulfilled!"

Sujata leaned forward. "Seeing you today, in the van, you looked so free and confident. I'll never forget you marching out of Wagamamas. I wanted to run after you and escape too. I've been questioning my choices ever since, wondering how I ended up in a glass prison in Canary Wharf."

"A caged canary!" Tim laughed.

"Well, yes!" she agreed. "But seriously, I got swept up in doing what my folks expected. Going to Uni, getting a good job, settling down. It all seems hollow and pointless now. Last autumn, my cousin Yogini started working in an orphanage in Slovakia – it's full of Roma children and they're desperate for volunteers. Yogini says the kids live in squalor – I'm thinking of going there next year."

A waiter turned up the background music. A sitar repeated a series of notes over and over, deepening in intensity. Sujata's dark hair gleamed in the candlelight, and Tim wanted to run his finger across the delicate curve of her cheekbone.

"I wonder if they eat toffee apples in Slovakia," he said. He reached out and took her hand.

Pushkin and the Gypsy

Snow was falling.

Zemfira stood in the square, gazing up at the statue, eating a piece of cake she'd found on a park bench. Sensing someone behind her, she turned round. It was Old Viktor.

"Ah, my child," Viktor said in a funny, dreamy voice. "That's our Pushkin. Alexander Sergeivich Pushkin, the greatest poet in the world! Beloved by Tsars and peasants alike. Wrote about your people too, had great empathy for Gypsies, being as how he was black himself."

Zemfira stared at Viktor in surprise. She looked up at Pushkin's head again, although her neck was getting stiff. The kind granite face towered above her.

"Yes," Viktor continued, "one of Pushkin's poems is even called *The Gypsies*. It starts like this." Taking a deep breath, the old man declaimed, "A group of Gypsies roams through Bessarabia, a fire burns, a family prepares food, everything is peaceful, the moon shines....."

His voice boomed in the frosty air as words steamed from his mouth, rising upwards to wreath Pushkin's head. "I can't remember the verse properly. I studied literature at University, you know, but my memory isn't so good these days." He scratched his head. "Come to think of it, the beautiful heroine was called Zemfira, just like you!"

He hobbled back through the snow to join his friends at the open-air chess table.

"It doesn't make sense," Zemfira told the statue. "So you're a famous poet, beloved by Tsars and peasants alike. I understand why they want to remember you – Russians love poetry – but Viktor Alexandrovich says you're black!"

She laid a sympathetic hand on Pushkin's foot. "Lots of Russians hate black people, so how come everyone loves you? A black poet? How come they adore you so much they put up a statute of you in every park and square?"

She straightened with pride. This man, this Pushkin, was a Gypsy, just like her! He'd even written a poem about a girl called Zemfira, just like her.

"I make up poems too," she confided to the stone poet. "Begging poems, I call them. But no one loves me. When I was nine, my stepmother took me out of school. Now I have to clean the house and look after her kids. She sends me into the streets to beg. Sometimes the Russian children sneer at me, because I wear a long skirt and a scarf. They jeer at my dark skin."

She brushed cake crumbs from her clothes, smoothing down her skirt. "Maybe you're wondering how come I know Viktor. Well, one day, some brats were shouting at me, just as Viktor was passing my pitch. He chased them off, and brought me to the square to meet his friends. Now I come here every day. The old men let me watch them play chess. They share their food with me, biscuits or fudge. All their grandchildren live in other countries, in Holland or America or England, so they call me their granddaughter. No one at home knows I mix with the *Gadje*, and even if they did, no one would care. Only my Dada cared about me, and he's been dead for three years."

Zemfira coughed and pulled her shawl tighter round her thin shoulders. She wanted to cry. Pushkin stood calm, firm, unmoving.

Zemfira cleared her throat. "My Dada used to be an actor with the Kalinin Gypsy Theatre Company. I still remember how he used to talk about it." She deepened her voice, mimicking her father. "Salary paid by the State. Performances all over the Soviet Union. Visits to Kazakhstan, Siberia, Georgia. To Latvia and Poland. Staying in hotels or with Gypsy comrades. Food and work guaranteed."

Zemfira blew on her cold fingers, slipping her hands beneath her shawl. "But after that old Gorbachov and Boris Yeltsin took over, after *perestroika,* there was no more government money for *Romani* culture. Everything changed, even the name of our town. In Communist times it was known as Kalinin. Now it's called Tver! We were happy in Kalinin, but in Tver everything is sad. So, Dada had to go to Germany to work on a building site. There he caught pneumonia. Now he's dead. I've only got a wicked stepmother who hits me if I work too slowly. Or if I don't bring her enough money!"

"Zemfira, we're going to the market, see you later!" called the chess players as they left the square.

Zemfira waved at them. She was enjoying talking to Pushkin. He didn't interrupt, or fidget, or say she was talking rubbish. "I come here every day now. This square is my refuge. I spend the morning begging at the bus station, then I take a break in the square. Viktor and his comrades sit round the open-air chess table over there. Petrov brings the chessmen, Igor is in charge of food and Viktor provides flasks of tea. Sometimes someone brings *samogon* but they don't let me drink any. They say I'm too young to drink spirits. Then they all get very happy, and Petrov falls asleep. They like the square too, they're all retired, you see, and live in tiny rooms. This freezing park is their refuge too."

A gust of wind blew snow into Zemfira's face. "Viktor says this is the hardest winter for sixty years. I hate the winter, the streets are so slippery and everyone's bad tempered." She sighed, and touched Pushkin's shoe. "I've got to go to work the lunchtime rush, but I'll come back this afternoon."

Pushkin stared ahead, squinting through the driving sleet.

Jumping over snowdrifts and icy puddles, Zemfira hurried to her pitch at the Bus Station. Baba Maria nodded cheerfully from behind her cardboard box of pickled onions and shrivelled turnips. Uncle Ivan was playing his *bayan*, his cold hands slipping over the keys. Zemfira took her place between her friends, trying to tap her toes in time to the music, but her feet were too numb to move.

This must be how my statue feels, she thought. Frozen. Icy. Stone.

She tried out one of her new begging poems in a high, ringing voice.

"Spare a coin, brother, God will bless you.
Sister, give a kopek to a poor Gypsy girl.
My parents are dead.
I'm a starving orphan with a wicked stepmother.
She will beat me if I don't earn enough money.
She will pull my hair.
She will pinch me.
I'm ten years old.
My little foot is numb with cold.
Bitter snow seeps through my leaking shoe."

An old man pressed a coin into her hand, and a handsome student stopped to listen to her chant and gave her a kopek.

"Gypsy, dirty Gypsy! Here's some change for you!" A sharp stone struck Zemfira's arm and she cowered behind Baba Maria's box, trying to shield her body from the hail of pebbles. A gang of children surrounded her, faces twisted with scorn.

"Leave her alone!" yelled a familiar voice. Viktor Alexandrovich and his comrades rushed up, shaking their walking sticks like bayonets.

"Perverts!" sneered the boys. "You can keep your smelly *tsiganka*!"

As the old men closed in, the youngsters ran away laughing.

"Fascists! We fought to free our Fatherland from monsters like you," Petrov shouted after them.

Viktor put his hand on Zemfira's shoulder. "You look so cold, *milaya*. Come and sit with us for a while. You're too young to be working so hard."

Her heart thudded like an axe on wood, sweat frosted her forehead. Her arm hurt. Thrusting the moneybag beneath her ragged shawl, she followed Viktor back to the square. The chess players sat her down, fussing over her. Petrov poured a glass of hot tea, checking her pulse while she drank. Igor, an ex-surgeon, examined her arm and cleaned the wound.

Lowering himself heavily onto the bench, Viktor rummaged in his pocket, drawing out a screw of paper. "Help yourselves," he said, pouring black and white sunflower seeds onto the chess board. Then he picked up a tiny seed, examining it closely. "It's strange how something so small, so drab, can produce a plant as dramatic and exotic as a golden sunflower."

"I like the way you talk," Zemfira told him, her breath curling away. "My father used to talk like you. Like a poet. That's because he was a Gypsy, like our Pushkin."

Viktor looked surprised. "Bless you, child! Our Pushkin wasn't a Gypsy. Whatever gave you that idea?"

A cold hole carved into Zemfira's stomach. "But you said…... Pushkin was black, he lived with the Gypsies. He wrote about a girl called Zemfira. He loved……"

"No, no, *darogaya*, you've got hold of the wrong end of the stick. He was black because his ancestors came from Abyssinia. That's in Africa, you know. His great-grandfather was an African prince, so they say, kidnapped by Turks and sent to the Royal Household of Russia. Our great poet, Alexander Sergeivich Pushkin, lived in the Palace, he was a courtier to the Tsar. He went to University, he was an aristocrat."

Zemfira's hand trembled. Tea spilled onto her skirt, darkening the fabric. Absently she wiped the drops away with her hand. The tea is the same colour as my skin, she thought.

She licked the liquid from her fingers, tasting the sugar.

She shook her head. Viktor must have made a mistake. Just because he'd been to University didn't mean he knew everything. She stood up, brushing sunflower husks from her ragged skirt. A little bird hopped up and pecked at the empty shells.

"Thank you for the seeds, Viktor Alexandrovich," Zemfira said politely.

"Come tomorrow, Zemfira. My wife is cooking *pirogi*. I'll bring some for you."

Petrov set out chess pieces for another game.

Zemfira slung her bag of coins round her neck. She started to walk through the square, back to the bus station, dreading another afternoon begging on the freezing street.

As she passed the statue, she glanced up at Pushkin's face. A pigeon was perched on the poet's head, staring out at the town. Pushkin's kind eyes looked down at her. He was smiling. *"Sar san, chay? Sar trais tu?"* he asked.

Zemfira laughed. Pushkin was speaking *Romanes*. She was right. She'd known all along he was a Gypsy. She imagined running away with him, the wheels of their caravan scrawling poems over the snowy wastes of Bessarabia. Pushkin's dark face would glow as he recited verses to her around the fire at night. He probably played the violin too, like Dada. She'd be safe with him. His strong arms would protect her.

Climbing nimbly up the stone figure, she nestled to his chest. Pushkin embraced her, warming her cold body. She clung to him, melting into him.

And then she began to sing.

Not for money, but for the love of singing.

A flock of pigeons flew above her, flapping their wings in time to her music.

The melody rang round the park, over the snowy town.

Glossary

Dada – Dad   (*Romani*)

perestroika – restructuring [refers to end of Communist era]
(Russian)

samogon – homemade vodka   (Russian)

milaya – sweet girl   (Russian)

daragaya – my dear   (Russian)

pirogi – little pies   (Russian)

bayan – button accordion   (Russian)

tsiganka – Gypsy   (Russian)

Sar san, chay? Sar trais tu? – How are you, girl?   (*Romani*)

Dear Chingiz

I'm sitting at the computer, staring at the blank screen. I can't believe it! Me, retiring! Finished! Most of my friends moan about their work, but I enjoy College life, the energy of my students and the eccentricities of my colleagues.

Although my grandchildren treat me as if I'm simple, rolling their eyes when I ask about You Tube, or want to analyse the lyrics of the inane pop songs they constantly sing, I still feel young. Only when I'm shaving, and see my bald head and wrinkled skin in the mirror, do I remember that I really am sixty-five.

I glance at the screen, hoping it might have magically filled itself up in the last few minutes, but it's still blank. What can I talk about? Speeches are usually so boring, and I don't want to come out with a load of platitudes like George did at his leaving do.

George, former Head of the IT Department, retired at Christmas, and at the small reception held in his honour, he'd banged on about how education and college conditions had changed for the better, and how he knew his colleagues had great hopes for the future.

He's wrong there! I have no hope for the future at all. Things can only get worse, what with all the restructuring and the cuts. Standards are falling, half the students in mainstream classes can't read or write properly, and many of them are rude and demanding. At least when I began my teaching career, almost all my pupils were polite and grateful.

Rain lashes the window, and in the street outside, a car splashes through a puddle, drenching an old woman. She stands on the pavement, shaking her umbrella at the driver.

The rain stops as suddenly as it began, and a weak ray of sunshine falls on my face. I gaze into the computer screen, willing some inspiration to come from its depths. And eerily, from the pearly whiteness, a face emerges. A weather-beaten face with angry grey eyes and a black moustache. Bertie.

Bertie had been a student in the first Adult Literacy Class I taught, just over forty years ago. Unpredictable and moody, he moved like a cat, silently and with hidden menace. College records revealed he had just been housed after years spent travelling round Kent with his Gypsy family. Recently widowed, he now lived in London with a grown up daughter. It was this daughter who had enrolled him on the literacy course.

All the other students made an effort in the lessons, squinting at the letters and guessing at words they didn't know, but Bertie always turned towards the window, watching the sky and twirling a pencil in his strong fingers, refusing to join in.

The memory of those days is so strong, my fingers move to the keyboard of their own accord and begin to type a speech, words flying onto the screen as I recall my strange, angry student.

It was my first year as a teacher, and the slogans from St. Giles College were still fresh in my mind. "Let the students know you like them! Show them you care."

I had never met any Gypsies, learning the little I knew about them from newspaper reports and television programmes. They were usually portrayed as an exotic and somewhat aggressive people. But I considered myself to be a tolerant person, so, one lunchtime, instead of going straight to the staffroom, I asked Bertie to stay behind for a chat.

"Don't you want to learn to read?" I said bluntly.

Bertie looked at the desk, rubbing his hand over the laminated surface. The edging strip was coming away, and he tugged at it. "Needs gluing back!" he commented. "Shameful how folks let things go!"

He stretched out his legs and shifted in his seat. "No need to read," he said. "But I tells you what. I'd like to learn to write."

I glanced at him. "Why do you want to write?"

"Want to write a letter." After a short silence, he added, "To Chingiz Aitmatov."

For a moment I stared at him in surprise. "Aitmatov?" I repeated. "How do you know about Aitmatov?"

Bertie bristled. "Why shouldn't I know about him? Think just because I'm a Gypsy I don't know nothing? That I'm an ignorant old fool? I know his book Farewell Gulsari *off by heart!" And to prove his point, he rattled off the first sentence of the book. "An old man and an old horse...."*

I hurriedly interrupted. "No, no, of course I don't think you're ignorant. Only he's my favourite author too, and hardly anyone in England has ever heard of him. I'm simply pleased to find another fan."

Bertie stood up, half smiling. When he wasn't scowling, his face was handsome. I got up too. "I'll help you write a letter," I told him. "We'll send it to him, and if you keep coming to class, you'll be able to read his reply. Can you stay behind after tomorrow's lesson?"

In class the following day, I was pleased to see Bertie pick up his pencil and copy some words from the board. When the other students left, Bertie sat next to me and dictated his letter. He said it straight out, from the heart, as if he was alone with Aitmatov

"Dear Chingiz," *he began.* "I'm getting in touch because I want to let you know I really rate your book, *Farewell Gulsari*. I live in England and you're from Central Asia, but it's like you're writing about me and my life. I specially like the way you get into the spirit of the horse. I used to ride a horse meself, but now we live in Brixton, I've only got a dog.

"I like the way you write about the steppes. It's hard for me to picture wide-open spaces where you can wander for miles without ever meeting a living soul. Here in London we live on top of each other, and even in the countryside there's always someone around, a farm worker for example, or a farmer telling you to clear off his land. Or the *gavvers*, the police, moving you on.

"To be honest with you, the man in your book – I can't remember his name – he's a bit like me. The one everyone disagrees with, although he's a really top bloke, a grafter what tells the truth. And for some reason, it's the same for me! I dunno why, but I seems to get up people's noses!"

I wanted to tell Bertie that he looked so angry, he scared people, but I didn't. He gave me a funny look, as if he knew what I was thinking. "What's the name of that bloke in the book?" he snapped. "You said you've read it too."

"I can't remember," I confessed. "Wasn't he just called 'the man' – as if he was so downtrodden he didn't deserve a name?"

"Mebbe," Bertie grunted. "But I'm sure he did have a name. I've just gone and forgot it."

Clearing his throat he dictated some more.

"That's why I like your book, Chingiz. Your *mush*, your geezer, he works hard and does what he's told even when he knows the boss is wrong. And who gets the blame when it all blows up? He does, don't he!

"Puts me in mind of the time I was working on the buildings, and told the boss about them paints he bought.

66

They never covered the wood proper, but he said, 'Shut up, Bertie; I got 'em cheap down the market, it'll be okay.' Then the paint sort of curdles, like that time your man's trying to mend the tent, *yurt*, I think he calls it in his language; well I know he never painted it, but he ain't got the right materials to mend it and of course, he gets the blame when it falls down. And me, I gets the blame for the bad paint job."

I put down the pen to rest my stiff hand. "The yurt is the oldest transportable house in the world," I said. "Older than the caravan."

"I knows that!" Bertie scoffed. "The caravan's quite a modern invention. Why, in the old days, people used tents or benders. But them yurts sound like a good idea, when they're in good nick, mind. You ready to go again?"

Although I wanted to ask what a bender was, I was reluctant to interrupt, so I nodded and he continued.

"And in winter, when all the sheep are dying 'cos there's no fodder for 'em, his boss gives him a right rollicking and your *mush,* he never says nothin, 'cos he knows no one'll listen to him and he ain't got the words and he's freezing cold and knackered from working all day. That weren't right. Your man never went to college and his fat educated boss stands in front of him in a warm fur coat, while your bloke is starving and hard of words.

"Tell you the truth, Chingiz, I was hoping your man would say, 'It's your fault; you never help me. Your life is sorted and you live in the village in a nice house. You stole Gulsari, my horse. You sent us to live in the mountains in this mouldy old *yurt* and the rain comes in and me old lady gives me jip because the nippers are always ill.' But no, he just stands there and takes it.

"Chingiz, you must be asking how come a bloke in Brixton who never finished school read your book. Tell the truth, I ain't actually read it, but our Laura's told me all about it. Laura's the daughter. She finished University, did Russian and Business Studies – they're all doing Business Studies now. I expect it's the same where you come from.

"Anyways, one summer she translates your book for me when we're in Wales. Wales is in Great Britain, sort of on the left of London and underneath Scotland, it's got mountains and lakes. Must be a bit like Kyrgyzstan, come to think of it.

"One day it's pouring with rain, and the wife goes off with Pete, our boy, to Cardiff for the day, and me and the girl was sitting in the trailer waiting for the rain to stop – like that bit in your book when the rain just comes down in the mountains like the end of the world. So I makes us a cuppa and my Laura says, 'Tell you what, Dad, I've got this Russian book with me; we're studying it at Uni. Why don't I translate a bit for you, you'll really like it.'"

I needed a break, so I went to the canteen to get some tea from the Automat. I was surprised to learn Bertie's daughter was a graduate. As I've mentioned already, I didn't know much about English Romanies at the time, so the idea of a well-educated one, especially a girl, astonished me.

Bertie was pacing round the classroom, throwing out his legs in that strange way of walking he has. He insisted on paying for the drinks, taking a long swig from his cup, bending his neck right back.

Eager to learn more about his life, I picked up the pen and reminded him where he'd got to. "Laura's just gone to get the book."

"Right," he says, "let me think; what happened next? Okay, write this."

"She fetches the book and starts translating it into English, stumbling over some words, but I gets the meaning. I like the way it begins with the old man and the *grai* walking along the road, clopping along real slow and the man talking to the horse and then the horse can't go no further. Then there's this sort of flashback over his life, showing how the horse used to be free and run around the mountains with its herd.

"Chingiz, it got me remembering how I used to be free too. When I was little we stopped in Kent on a smallholding for a couple of years, on a little farm. Me dad had *Romani* blood, he traded horses and me mum kept chickens and we all mucked in, all the *chavies*, the kiddies. It was real *kushti*, looking after all the animals and being out in the rain and mud. I learned to ride as a *tikno*, a boy, just like your man. Was good too, could ride without a saddle and used to trot the horses up and down the racing track at fairs."

How I envied the life Bertie was describing. I'd been raised in West Kensington by a stern Bulgarian father and an aristocratic mother. My childhood had been one of study and obedience.

"Laura says your horse and your man lost their freedom. She says when Gulsari was captured and gelded, he lost his liberty, and your man was kept down by his lack of education and the system, so he was gelded too. Well, not really of course, but it's a symbol, Laura says."

At this point, Bertie changed from an amiable storyteller dictating a letter, into an angry student. His eyes blazed and his cheeks darkened. He began to talk louder, as if addressing a meeting of Militant Socialists.

"I tells yer, Chingiz, when the daughter said that about the gelding, it made me think. See, it's no different here, in England. I got to tell yer, Chingiz, they say everyone's equal in Britain, but don't you believe it! All the folk what's done well and got on in life, when you check it out, they've all got some power behind them, every one of them! Sometimes you see some daft *rakli* or bloke on tele, and you thinks, what the hell they doing on there? And it turns out their dad's Sir somebody or other, or their Ma's a famous actress. Yes, it seems to me that if you ain't got some dosh behind yer, or some kind of power, you might as well give up."

I gulped. The man I'd subconsciously assumed was an ignorant Gypsy had just neatly described the British class system and celebrity culture.
"Write this!" he ordered.

"My Laura, she's going to break in on her own merit. A few people do. Not many though. She's the first of our family to get an education and we're right proud of her, and she ain't turned out posh or nothing, just the same old Laura. Her brother Pete, though, our boy, he's another kettle of fish! Won't get his hands dirty, and that's another thing like in your book. Your old man's son – off he goes to the nearest town to work on the black market. Our Pete's always down the clubs, wheeling and dealing. He's what we call a wide boy, up to all the tricks."

Bertie stopped and held out a packet of cigarettes. Although we weren't allowed to smoke on College premises, I accepted the fag and we lit up, using our empty cups as ashtrays. When I opened the window to get rid of the smell, the cold London air blew into the classroom, laced with a tang of petrol.

Bertie breathed out a wisp of smoke and looked over to see if I was ready. I flicked my dog-end out of the window and sat down again.

"It's not all the lad's fault, I know. In the old days, us Travellers could always earn a bit of *vongar* – there was the farm work and the fairs and the peddling. Enjoyed that as kids; going from door to door with pegs, or sharpening knives, or selling wooden flowers with Ma. Some of the village people was right *kushti*, give us kids biscuits or big lumps of cheese.

"All changed now, of course. Nowhere to stop, see. Councils don't let you stay in fields no more, and the villagers get up in arms when Travellers come along wanting to pull in for a night or two. And now the farms got so big and use machinery, they don't need no help picking hops or cherries. And if they do, they use people from down your neck of the woods – Poles and Ukrainians and Chinese – cheaper, see.

"And I tell you what, it's like living in a prison, where I live now. The house is nice enough, got all the facilities, but I'm used to living in the open, see. When you live in a trailer you're in the middle of nature – you can pull off when you want and stop where you want. Well, you can't now, but that's what it was like when I was a boy. Laura lives on the third floor of this block, and I've never bin in a house with stairs before. Feel caged in and desperate. But I don't let on to me daughter. That's why I come to these classes, get out from under her feet and I can look at the trees outside the classroom window.

"What I wanted to say, Chingiz, is, if ever you find yourself in our parts, pop round for a cup of tea. Do you drink tea? I know your man drinks it with ewe's milk. I'll ask Ali from the Turkish shop in the High Street if he can lay his hands on some ewe's milk.

"I'd love to have a chinwag with yer. I know you're busy, being an ambassador and a writer and all, but you'd be very welcome. Drop us a line.

70

"So, all the best from me, a faithful reader. Well, not exactly a reader, not yet anyway, more of a listener.
Bertie Smith."

Bertie walked over to the window and stared out at the cloudy sky. Then he turned, smiling, and held out his hand for the handwritten letter. "Thanks, Emil," he said. "I'll get Laura to translate this into Russian and type it up. Then I'll get her to send it to the Russian Embassy in London. And I will keep on with your lessons, the writing and reading, so when Chingiz replies, I'll be able to read his answer."

Bertie came to a few more lessons, but then he dropped out. So I don't know if Chingiz Aitmatov ever replied to him. And now both men are dead. But because of people like Bertie, teaching literacy and language skills has been a great career, bringing me huge challenges and huge rewards. Thanks to Bertie I realised that Gypsies were no more exotic or frightening than any other group. Meeting him forced me to examine prejudices I didn't even know I had, and I learnt as much from him as he did from me. And that's the true meaning and purpose of education!

I lean back and take a deep breath, looking at my watch. To my surprise, I've been typing for over an hour. The sky is a misty blue-grey with the afternoon sun hanging low over the houses opposite. My back aches from bending over the keyboard.

"Not bad for a retirement speech," I congratulate myself, saving the file. "That'll make them think! Just needs a bit of tidying up and editing and it'll be ready. I'll try it out on Theresa tonight, after we've eaten."

Switching off the computer, I go into the kitchen to fix the evening meal.

Glossary

gavvers – police   (*Romani*)

mush – man   (*Romani*)

bender – a Traveller tent – canvas or blankets stretched over bent sticks
or rods.

yurt – portable construction   (Kyrgyz)

grai – horse   (*Romani*)

chavies – children   (*Romani*)

kushti – good/nice   (*Romani*)

tikno – lad   (*Romani*)

rakli – girl   (*Romani*)

vongar – money   (*Romani*)

Sainte Sara's Babe

A white stallion neighs from a nearby pasture, raising its head as the riders pass by.

Esmeralda tightens Bonheur's reins and follows Antonio along the sandy road. A flock of pink flamingos wings above her, welcoming her to the Camargue.

The horses clop southwards to the distant town. Tooting cars pass, full of waving *Gens du passage*. Trailers rock precariously as drivers swerve round the horses, familiar faces smiling through windows before rushing onwards.

Esmeralda and her husband continue on their way, making for the clump of trees next to the brook. Antonio leaps from Sauvage and tethers the horse to a tree. As Esmeralda slips off Bonheur, the docile mare bends to graze on the lush grass.

Esmeralda and Antonio walk down to the riverbank. Esmeralda re-plaits her thick brown hair, stoops and washes her hands, splashing her face. Cool water trickles down her neck, drips onto her blouse. She turns to her husband, treasuring this golden moment of sun and solitude.

Antonio wraps his arms around her, pressing her into his lean body. A bee buzzes round Esmeralda's head. Antonio grasps her thin shoulders, a gleam in his green eyes. "This time, *Sainte Sara* will grant our wish. I feel it."

Esmeralda wants to believe him. She nods and walks back to the trees to unpack the *panier*. She spreads a cloth under the shady branches and gets out the provisions. As she unwraps the pizza, the smell of strong cheese makes her eyes water. There's a humming in her ears, and for a moment she thinks she's going to faint. She wipes the sweat from her forehead, watching Antonio light a small fire and boil the camping kettle.

The distant hum of traffic throbs in the background. Bonheur trots up to Sauvage and nuzzles him. Sauvage whinnies and lays his head on Bonheur's flank.

Steam wisps into the afternoon blue of the sky. Antonio spoons coffee and sugar into cups, stirs in boiling water, hands Esmeralda her drink. She sips, leaning against the tree, sighing with contentment.

"We'll be lucky this year, Sainte Sara will grant our wish. *Tante* Ana said she could see it in the stars."

Antonio pulls Esmeralda to her feet. He kisses her forehead.
"They'll be waiting for us. We better get going or it'll be night before
we arrive."

Esmeralda nods and takes a shawl from her bag, tying it round her
shoulders. The couple remount, and the horses pick their way along
the twilight tracks. As they trot along the coastal road, they hear
singing from the *terraine*, and the horses quicken pace, sensing the
journey is almost over. Lights from caravans gleam in the camping
area, small fires are blazing all over the field. Musicians are tuning up,
practising riffs, shadowy figures twirl to the music. Laughing children
run around, calling to each other.

A mist passes across Esmeralda's eyes. The darkness distorts the
scene, lengthening the figures into strange shapes and postures.
Antonio jumps easily from his horse, but she cannot move.

A familiar voice claims her.

"Welcome! Esmeralda, Antonio, come eat and drink! You must
be tired from the journey."

Her aunt's greeting slices away the tiredness, and Esmeralda
dismounts. Her mother, sisters, brothers and cousins hug her, shouting
and laughing.

Soon she's by the fire with a plate of stew and a mug of strong
coffee. After a few mouthfuls, Esmeralda leans against her mother and
stares at the flames. This camping ground is an island in a stormy sea,
a place of refuge and affirmation. No one will come to move the
Travellers on. No one will throw stones. No mobs will destroy their
caravans. Not tonight. Not during the pilgrimage of Sainte Sara, the
patron saint of the *Gens du voyage*.

Oncle Pablo thrusts a guitar into Antonio's hands. "Tune up!" he
commands. "Come on, Esmeralda. We need to practice! We've not
played together since Christmas – we don't want to let ourselves
down."

Slinging a heavy accordion over his broad shoulders, Pablo plays a
chord and hums the melody line of *Lili Lili*, while Antonio tunes the
guitar.

Antonio picks out the song, embellishing it with ornaments and
trills. *Tante* Ana jumps up, fluttering her fingers, arms stretched to the
sky. Esmeralda joins her, exhaustion leaving her body as she follows
Ana's movements. She feels the spirit enter her as her cousins clap
and shout encouragement.

Later, Pablo assigns the family tasks for the following day. "You
boys will tend the horses. Musicians, set up at the church. Ana, you're

in charge of selling medals to the tourists. Isabelle, take a group to the market place to sell the goods."

Although Esmeralda rises early next day, fires are already burning all over the encampment. Different dialects mingle with the noise of barking dogs and crying babies.

She turns to the rising sun. *"Chère Sara, toi la sainte patronne des voyageurs et gitans du monde entier,* hear my prayer. I am already twenty-one, and long for a child. Smile on me, I beg you, and grant my wish!"

A coral streak cleaves the sky as a lone flamingo, hurrying to catch up with the rest of the flock, flies over Esmeralda's head.

Tante Ana shares out the stock of tin medals, pouring them into plastic bags. Each medal is embossed with an image of Sainte Sara and a picture of the church of Notre Dame de la Mer.

"Remember to smile at the visitors! We must sell everything!" *Tante* Ana encourages the women. "We need to buy food and petrol for the journey home. It was quiet yesterday, may Sainte Sara give us a better day today."

Esmeralda walks with her mother and aunt down to the town square, greeting friends and relations trooping along the dusty road. "Hey, Esmeralda!" calls Blieta, a friend from Holland. "When you coming back to Roermond?"

Esmeralda smiles. "Maybe in autumn," she replies, staring at the beautiful dark-haired baby in Blieta's arms. Children are everywhere, babies suckling under shawls, toddlers running and laughing and shouting. Her sisters and brothers are already parents. There's an agonising ache in her soul.

A Mercedes races by, hooting frantically, forcing the pedestrians onto the pavement. "Clear off, you rich Serbians! Mafia, the lot of you!" shouts *Tante* Ana, shaking her fist. "No manners, these Yugoslavian Gypsies! Just because some of them went to University, they think they're a cut above the rest of us!"

Everyone laughs. Esmeralda's laugh dries in her throat as Blieta thrusts her little boy into her arms. "He's two months!" Blieta says. "He's my life, my king, my treasure."

Esmeralda sighs with longing as she strokes the baby's soft golden cheek. The child gives a gummy smile and grasps her finger in his fist, pulling it into his mouth. He sucks rhythmically, smacking his lips.

At stalls along the main road, women in festive costumes are unpacking their wares. In the church courtyard, Pablo and his group have already set up the instruments, and are checking the sound system. Around the forecourt, other groups are arranging stools and adjusting amps, strumming softly, tightening strings.

Ana places the women at strategic places around the square.

"I hope we get the sunny spot by the oak with the benches, so we can sit down," Esmeralda says to her sister-in-law Amarita.

Amarita spits on the ground, balancing baby Carlos on her hip. "Joking, aren't you? She always gives that place to her daughters! The likes of us'll be hawking along *rue de la Charotte*, where all the restaurants are. Ana's always going on about the Serbian Mafia, but she's just as bad!"

Esmeralda groans. Restaurants are the worst places for hawking. The hungry diners are too busy studying the menu before they eat. And after they've had a meal and paid, they're too full and too poor to open their wallets again.

As they wait for hotel guests to finish breakfast and wander into town, Esmeralda and Amarita play with Carlos, taking turns to carry the gurgling infant.

Amarita jabs Esmeralda's arm. "Look! Here's a likely couple. You take first pick of the day. It'll bring you luck."

A middle-aged couple are strolling down the street, talking loudly in French. The woman looks gentle and the man has a friendly smile.

Esmeralda pulls her shawl round her shoulders, opens the bag of badges with a dazzling grin. *"Une médaille, ma belle*? You have a kind face – Sainte Sara will bless you, she will bring you great fortune."

The woman hesitates, hands fluttering over her purse. She looks at Esmeralda, then at her husband.

"Mais non, Claire!" the man says. "You've already got five of those tin things! What do you need another one for?"

Claire shrugs apologetically and follows her husband along the street to the sea front.

"Damn!" swears Esmeralda. "Now I'll have Ana scolding me tonight."

"Hold Carlos!" commands Amarita. "I'll take the next lot."

Some teenagers are running along the road, laughing and shouting. Amarita jumps in front of the giggling gang.

"Eh, mes enfants, prenez une médaille! Sainte Sara vous bénisse!"

Coins clink into the moneybag, and Amarita returns triumphant. Now a few Americans wander down the street, wearing bright Bermuda shorts and weighed down with video equipment. They film Esmeralda and Amarita, stuff wads of euros into their hands. Esmeralda takes the money, feeling uncomfortable. Her picture will travel across the seas to be gawped at by strangers.

At midday, she buys some *friand de fromage* from the charcuterie behind the church. They walk across to the sea front, and Amarita lays her sleeping son on a shawl while they eat. Then they wash their hands in the sea and rearrange their hair, the breeze cooling their cheeks.

"I wish we could stay here all day," sighs Amarita, wiping traces of sand from her son's hair.

"In your dreams!" Esmeralda replies. She feels drugged and disembodied, as if she really is in a dream.

The long day crawls towards afternoon. The tourists go back to their hotels to rest. Esmeralda feels sad and tired. She's been up since six o'clock, washing clothes and cooking. She's been out on the streets all day. She's had enough of selling useless bits of tin to tourists who don't want them. She's not like the others – she doesn't enjoy the challenge of charming money out of holidaymakers.

In small groups, the *Gens du voyage* straggle back to the encampment. Time for the evening meal, time to put on their best costumes. Esmeralda stops at the town fountain to wash her face. She gulps mouthfuls of water and dries her fingers on her hair.

The first star gleams above Notre Dame de la Mer. In a new frock of deep blue silk, a flowered Spanish shawl over her head, Esmeralda follows her husband into the church. This year, it's the turn of Antonio's family to perform at the feet of Sainte Sara, and Esmeralda has been chosen to sing in the tiny crypt. In her hands is the satin scarf she embroidered during the winter months, the delicate material decorated with tiny sequins and beads. Before she sings, she will drape the scarf around the black statue of Sainte Sara in the smoky crypt.

The church is dark and cool. Esmeralda pauses in front of the two large figures of Sainte Marie Jacobe and Sainte Marie Salome. "Blessed Saintes," she mumbles, "you came to la Camargue two thousand years ago from *La Terre Sainte*, the Holy Land. In your small boat, you sailed with Sainte Sara across the sea to bring light to the people. Shine your holy light into me, I implore you!"

In front of the Saintes is the plaster model of a boat. The two Maries smile and point at the boat. Esmeralda looks down.

There, at the bottom of the boat, swaddled in soft muslin robes, lies a tiny, plump baby. The baby smacks its lips and gurgles. Esmeralda stretches out her hand. The baby grabs her finger and sucks it greedily, closing its eyes in pleasure.

"Come on, *chèrie*," Antonio says. "The others will have tuned up by now.""

Before Esmeralda turns away, she glances once more into the boat. It is empty. The two Saintes Maries are standing stiffly before her, their hands clasped in prayer.

Esmeralda follows her husband down the narrow stairs. She smoothes the soft offering against her chest, holds it to her heart.

In the crypt, draped in flickering shadows, Sara *la Kali* is waiting for her.

Glossary

Gens du passage – Travellers   (French)

Tante – Aunt   (French)

Oncle – Uncle   (French)

terraine – camping area   (French)

panier – basket   (French)

Gens du voyage – Travellers   (French)

friand de fromage – a cheesy snack   (French)

Chère Sara, toi la sainte patronne des voyageurs et gitans du monde entier – Dear Sara, Patron saint of all Travellers and Gypsies   (French)

Une medaille, ma belle? – a medal, my beauty?   (French)

Eh, mes enfants, prenez une médaille. Sainte Sara vous bénisse. – My children, take a medal. Saint Sara will bless you.   (French)

Chèrie – dear   (French)

la Kali – the black one   (*Romani*)

Song of the Fair

The colt backed nervously out of the horsebox.

"Mind out, lad!" its stocky owner warned Joey. "He'll kick you into the middle of next week if you're not careful!" The colt snorted, shook its head and sniffed the grass.

The field looked exactly the same as it had last year. Horseboxes were being unloaded, traders were unpacking cartons of goods, oilcloths were being spread over trestles.

As soon as Joey made his way back to the family stall, Ma handed him a box of china. "And don't drop it!" she warned. Ma always said that, although Joey never dropped anything. Not like his clumsy brother Mark. Joey could be trusted to arrange the cups on the display stand with the pictures facing neatly outwards to attract customers.

"I know what I'm doing, Ma," Joey replied. "Bin doing it long enough!"

Ma laughed and took another box of porcelain from the van. Lovely gold-rimmed plates from a dealer up in Yorkshire. That's where they spent summers, stopping with Dad's family, the Boswells. Every August, when they drove home to the Boreham Wood Site, the trailer was heavy with the weight of china, and Ma nagged Dad to drive carefully so nothing got broken.

Joey liked Barnet Horse Fair. First of all, he got the day off school. Lana, the lady from Traveller Services, explained to Joey's headmistress that it was good for his education. Second, he met up with relatives and friends he'd not seen since the previous year. Third, he could go over to the Traveller Education tent, and watch films and look at books and old photographs.

This year he had another reason for wanting to visit the Fair. There was a Singing Competition, and inside Joey's jacket, folded into neat quarters, was a song he'd written with Mark. He didn't expect they'd win, but if they did, they'd get a Certificate and fifty quid. Joey had written the words after hearing about Travellers in Italy and France getting chucked off their sites, and Mark had worked out the tune on his tin whistle.

Mark staggered up with another box of crockery from the trailer, and together the brothers unloaded the contents, arranging the dishes on racks. "Okay, lads," Ma said, handing Mark a tenner. "Have a look round now. Get yourselves something to drink and a bite to eat. And don't forget to bring me back a cup of tea!"

Joey chased after Mark. Between the booths, a man was step dancing on a wooden board, wobbling unsteadily as music blared from a sound system. "There's Uncle Bob," yelled Joey. Mark laughed. "He's had a few pints in The Misty Moon!"

The boys paused at the horse tack stall, examining riding crops and decorative buckles. Joey bought a glittery brooch for Ma from the jewellery table, then Mark stopped at a cardboard sign with LOUS BUTIQE scrawled on it. In front of the stall, on an iron clothes rack hammered into the ground, fancy jackets and shawls were swinging wildly in the wind. Mark tried on a red blazer.

"Some boutique," he joked, shaking the rack. A hanger slid forward, dropping a coat on the ground.

"You buying or not, young Mark," scolded Lou, peering out from behind the cardboard sign. "You pick that up quick, or I'll tell your Ma!"

They spent a long time at the ironwork table, admiring the weathervanes with cocks and horses that spun round in the wind. Mark wanted to buy something for Ma, but couldn't choose between a green horseshoe or a candlestick.

There was a rush of wind and the earth shook. "Mind your back!" someone yelled. Joey had strayed onto the trotters' track where bareback riders and trap drivers were wildly galloping up and down.

Mark pulled him out of the way, cuffing him round the head. "You do that every time, you do! You never learn! You'll get yourself *mullered* one day."

Shrugging Mark off, Joey pointed at the colt he'd seen that morning. The animal munched placidly as a group of gamblers threw dice nearby. Da, perched on an oil drum, raised a glass of beer and waved to his sons. The boys waved back.

"If we win the song competition, I'm going to buy that colt," Joey vowed.

Mark rolled his eyes. "Go on! We'll never win. Come on, Ma'll be gasping for her cuppa."

A long queue had formed at May's Refreshment Booth. Joey listened to the gossip, saving it up to tell Ma later on the journey back to Boreham. "His sister said he never got over the shock!" – "And then the *gavvers* come and *lelled* him, just like that!" – "He was *chorred*. Two 'undred he paid for it, he was that *motto*, never noticed it only had three legs!"

May's black eyes gleamed as she poured out the strong brown brew and added milk. "*Dordi*, you boys have grown! How you getting

on? Your Ma likes three sugars, right? And you'll be wanting a slab
of my coconut cake?"

ᏄᏆᏁᎢ

"Where've you bin? I'm fair parched!" complained Ma, grabbing
her drink. "I'm off to have a butchers now – your turn to mind the
stall!"

Joey grinned as Ma bustled off into the crowd. He liked selling.
"Finest cups!" he yelled. "Two for a fiver – none better this end of
England."

A lady in a smart dress examined the cups, checking for cracks and
running her fingers over the rim. "Nothing wrong with our wares,"
Joey assured her. "Only the best crockery from Boswell and Family."

The lady smiled. "And shouldn't you be at school, young man?
Learning to read and write? You need your education, plenty of time
for working when you're older. How old are you?"

Mark shot Joey a warning look, signalling that the woman might
be from Social Services. Tucking a lock of dark hair behind his ear,
Joey looked innocently at the lady. "How about a beautiful plate to go
with the cups, missus?" he asked. The woman chose a plate with a
picture of roses on it. Although Joey liked the plates with horses best,
he carefully wrapped her purchase in newspaper and handed it over.
"Good choice," he smiled, then he stooped to rummage in the boxes of
china till he was sure the woman had walked away.

At last Ma came back with bags of shopping. "Lana's asking after
you two. Get down to her tent, and if you see your Da on the way, tell
him to come and give me a hand."

Joey stopped to talk to the Lee brothers, stepping quickly aside
when a group of sisters swaggered by, gold earrings swinging as they
tossed their heads. "That *rakli* fancies you, Joey," teased Bob Lee.

It was true. The girl had winked at him. Her long blonde hair
swung in a ponytail as she flounced past, her tight silver shorts
sparkling in the sun. Her legs were fat and brown and she towered
above him, her plump stomach spilling out of her tee shirt.

Joey flushed and looked away. "Joey's got the hots for our Emmy-
May!" jeered his friends. Embarrassed, Joey slunk into Lana's tent.

The tent smelt of straw and sweat. Little kids were having their
faces painted, and Lana, surrounded by young children, was making a
model caravan.

"Come and join us," she called, holding out a brush dripping with
glue. Joey quickly walked past, heading for a circle of chairs where
someone was telling a story about a king, a wicked witch and a dragon.
Joey sat down to listen. It was an exciting story, and the storyteller,

Kate her name was, got the children to clap and stamp their feet to frighten away the witch.

When the tale was finished, Uncle Bob and an accordionist wandered into the tent. The accordionist played a Traveller song, and all the children screeched out the chorus. Uncle Bob, more steady on his feet now, got everyone up to dance a jig.

Lana poured glasses of juice and handed round biscuits. "In a few minutes we'll start the singing competition. All contestants line up over here so Kate can write down your names."

Excited children jostled to get to Kate, but Joey hung back, suddenly feeling sick. He never won anything, never even got third place. Mark was chatting up the girls at the craft table, munching a chocolate biscuit and drinking lemonade.

"I'm going back to the stall," Joey told him. "There's no point in making a fool of meself. You said we never stood a chance."

His brother shoved him impatiently. "I never meant it! You've got a great voice, and that's a *kushti* tune I wrote. Your words are good too. Just do your best. Go on, get in the queue."

Emmy-May crooned a country and western song about a cowboy dead on the lonesome prairie. A little boy sung a ballad about an Irish rebel. Pete Lee did a rock number, gyrating his hips as he belted out the tune.

It was Joey's turn. It was so stuffy in the tent he couldn't breathe. His mouth was dry. Mark played the introduction on the whistle. Joey opened his mouth but nothing came out. Mark stopped playing and hissed, "Go on!"

Mark played the introduction again. More girls pushed into the tent, sneering and giggling, but when Joey started to sing they fell silent. At first he sung so quietly, the audience strained to hear the words. When Joey realised people were really listening, he stood straighter, his voice strong and clear.

I am a Gypsy, I sat beneath the cross,
I stole a nail to protect the Boss.
They beat me and they whipped me, but the nail they couldn't find.
I'd hammered it so deep inside my mind.

Now all over Europe, I wander where I can,
Searching for a place to put my caravan.

They set their dogs upon me, they throw stones at my cart
And the freedom I treasure in my heart.

Has anyone got time left for us Travellers anywhere?
We're the jugglers in the circus, we're the hawkers at the fair.
They'll listen to the music, they'll stop to see the show,
But when the dancing's over, it's all, "Clear off! Time to go!"

We who are the Roma, we're the children of the Cross,
For He who hung upon it, yes, He's one of us.
I heard Him whisper softly when they burnt me with the Jew,
"Forgive them, Dadrus, every one, they know not what they do."

And in that far Hereafter, unless they change their ways,
They'll find that our sweet Father, our dear King of Days,
Will let us park our vardos just like in days of old,
While those who spurned His dearest folk, are left out in the cold."

The silence stretched on and on. Joey stared at the ground, wishing it would open up and swallow him. Then the audience was cheering and clapping, and Mark thumped Joey on the back. Lana and Kate huddled together, discussing the marks. After a few minutes Lana stood up.

"The judges have made their decision," she said. "It was a difficult task, and you were all absolutely brilliant and amazing. We've awarded third prize to Jonah from Hadwell Park Site. Jonah, come up and get your five pound book token." Jonah accepted the voucher and ran out of the tent shouting with joy.

"Second prize, a £10 voucher for Marks and Spencer, goes to Emmy-May for her lovely ballad." Wolf whistles and loud applause greeted Emmy-May as she swaggered forward to accept her prize.

"And the winner is........." Lana paused for so long, Joey's heart thudded in his chest. What if I have a heart attack, he thought. What if I die before I know who's won. "First prize for a great original song goes to Mark and Joey Boswell from Boreham Wood."

Mark hugged Joey and ruffled his hair. "Fifty quid!" he yelled. "Ma'll be really pleased."

A reporter from BBC Roaming Radio was waiting outside the tent. "Well done, boys! How did you come to write that?" she asked.

"You're very talented, that's a great song. What made you think that up?"

A black microphone was shoved in Joey's face, and his mind went blank. Mark, usually so confident and loud, looked at the muddy grass and shuffled his feet. "What gave you the idea?" prompted the reporter.

Joey looked up at the sky, at the birds flying overhead. "Well, me and Mark, we got upset when we heard about Gypsies in Italy and Romania and France getting beaten up and turfed off their *tans*. And then there's all them problems with Dale Farm in Essex. We didn't know what to do to help, so we thought we'd write a song. Mark's great at music and he made up the tune."

"And our Joey's always making up poems!" Mark added. "And one night, Granddad told us the legend of the Gypsy girl at the cross. You know, the girl who ran off with the nails, trying to save Jesus. And the next day we was walking to school and the song just sort of came."

The journalist nodded. "If your parents agree, will you lads come into the radio station on Sunday and sing your song live on air and tell us about the legend?"

A feeling of pride swept over Joey. He felt tall and handsome, a hero who was going to save the Roma nation. He saw himself riding through hills and forests on the white colt.

Emmy-May winked at him. "You can buy me a burger!" she said.

Glossary

mullered – killed   (*Romani*)

gavvers – police   (*Romani*)

lelled – taken away   (*Romani*)

chorred – robbed   (*Romani*)

Dordi – my goodness   (*Romani*)

rakli – girl   (*Romani*)

Dadrus – Father   (*Romani*)

vardo – caravan, trailer   (*Romani*)

tan – stopping place   (*Romani*)

Rosalita's Bunion

Rosalita stabbed another grip into her heavy oiled hair. The tight chignon pulled the skin of her temples, stretching her face into a drum. The pin of the red silk flower above her ear scratched like a thorn.

Dios! Such a humid evening. Sweat ran down her blouse, and she adjusted her scarlet shawl to hide the moisture beneath her armpits.

Her frilled black skirt was a circle of night, floating and swishing round her ankles as she moved. She could hear the tourists in the town square shouting impatiently for the performance to start. Like lions, she thought, waiting for their prey. She tossed her head, her long gold earrings tapping her neck.

Juan and Alejandro were laughing outside the dressing tent as they tuned up. Alejandro's strong fingers drummed the guitar, indicating the musicians were ready. Then Elmita slowly struck her hands together, quickening the sound to the rhythm of a racing heart.

As Carmela answered the claps in a syncopated echo, Elmita began to sing.

Rosalita eased her feet into her red lacquer shoes. The left shoe slipped on easily, but when she tried to put on the right, pain burnt through her toes.

Her sister's voice soared over the chatter of the spectators. *"Olé!"* yelled the audience, stamping their feet. Carmela gave several sharp, aggressive claps, a signal to Rosalita to hurry up.

Rosalita hooked the cord of the castanets over her thumbs, cushioning the dark wood in her sweaty palms. Pushing open the flap of the tent, she hobbled across the cobbles, her sore foot gradually accepting its agonising cage. As she approached the performance area, she straightened her back, swirling the train of her heavy skirt behind her.

Heat rose from the dusty square, parching her throat. Taking her place in front of the musicians, she lifted her arms, her fingers frozen like antlers.

I don't want to dance today! she thought, waiting for the music to change. I want to cut my hair short and wander round town in a flimsy dress like a tourist, wearing flip flops and licking ice-cream. I want to lie on the beach.

Eyes closed, she stood in front of the crowd.

Recently, some *payos* had come to the Gypsy quarter to speak to the women. There were some *Calí* too, part of an organisation, they said, to empower oppressed groups. These people, field workers they were called, came, asked questions, and wrote answers down in little black books. One of them had a tiny computer that worked on a battery. Then the field workers returned to the University of Granada, leaving Rosalita behind.

Juan quickened the tempo. Lazily, Rosalita moved her hands to another position, waiting mechanically for the next change of rhythm.

Until the field workers had visited, Rosalita hadn't known she was – what was the word – *marginada*; marginalised by society for being a *gitana*, denied decent education, accommodation and employment. And doubly marginalised, so Perlita, one of the young *Calí* had explained, by being a woman in a society which prided itself on *machismo*.

"I used to be like you," Perlita had told her. "Like you and your sisters. I was expected to fetch water, look after the younger children, cook, sing, dance. My life was controlled by men. But one day, I looked at my castanets, and realised they were like manacles, chaining me to the past. Someone taught me to read and write, and now I'm one of the first *gitanas* at Granada University. I'm studying sociology, you know."

After the researchers left, Elmita mimicked Perlita's academic speech. "I'm studying sociology, don't you know! My castanets are marginalised!"

"Thinks she's better than us. She's a traitor to her own people!" Carmela scoffed. Summing up what most of the others were saying, she added, "She's only a *zarzamora*, a blackberry in a suit!"

Although she couldn't help laughing at Elmita's impersonation of the field workers, Rosalita was confused and discontented. Was she really oppressed? There was so much love and teasing and laughter in her family. But there was also abuse when women didn't do as they were told, or when someone stepped out of line. When Lolita had wanted to go to College and study medicine, disputes had broken out in the community. Few *gitanos* ever moved out of the *barrio*, and for a girl to live as a student was unthinkable. Now Lolita was the mother of three young children, her face often bruised.

Last month, Rosalita had caught up with Lolita on the way to the shops. "You know those people who came to speak to us? The ones who talked about the struggle for equality? I want to learn to read properly. Will you teach me? I want to be like Perlita, strong and free!"

Lolita hadn't replied. She looked terrified and walked away. So Rosalita stopped asking questions. Yet now, all the time she was cooking or cleaning or chasing after the younger children, she was gored by a feeling of discontent.

"What's the matter with you?" nagged her mother. "You've grown so careless! You prick yourself when you sew sequins onto the costumes! You stumble when you dance! You used to be so neat and careful, you were the best dancer, but since those *payos* came you've changed!"

Rosalita knew that the tourists never noticed the blood stains on the satin, the bruises under the skirt. They saw only beautiful women in sequinned dresses which glittered in candlelit restaurants or beneath the moon in the *plaza*. They saw only strong, handsome men whose hands struck chords from guitars.

A gust of wind blew across the square, shaking the tiny lights strung between the trees. Rosalita drew herself up, circling her fingers as Alejandro slammed his hand down on the strings. Elmita began to sing again, a discordant wail that bounced off the small *casitas* and cafés round the square. Proudly, Rosalita lifted her head, holding her arms still. Carmela struck *palmas*, and Elmita's voice soared higher, echoing the guitar.

Rosalita lifted the folds of her skirt, revealing her shiny shoes. A sigh ran through the crowd as she thumped her heels in the *llamada*. Enraged by the pain in her foot, she quickened the drumming sound, losing herself in the torment. Twisting to face her mother, her heels beat a wordless accusation. 'I wanted to learn to read, but you said girls don't need to read.' Her feet moved like pistons in the *redoble*.

Now she was dominating the rhythm, and Juan glared at her, his fierce black eyes commanding her to slow down. Rosalita stared back at her husband, working her castanets in a thunderous *caretilla*. Like wooden birds, the castanets fluttered beneath her agile fingers as she tapped out her protest – *marginada, marginada, marginada!*

Throwing her arms above her head she stood stiffly for a moment, like an angry statue. 'I want to go to College, maybe work in an office! I want to wear a grey suit and a white silk blouse like Perlita!' she stamped. Raising her knee, she swung her leg to bring her foot down in front of her body, flicking out her skirt. Her arms whipped out, one resting on her stomach, the other behind her back. 'I'd like to walk round with friends in the evening, drink a *Cuba libre* in a bar.'

She'd seen them, the townsfolk and the tourists, spilling out onto the narrow streets, relaxing with their glasses of wine and their happy smiles. They looked so young, so free.

Turning her head to the side, she snaked her arm outwards, scornfully clicking her castanets at the eager spectators. 'And you, if I was still a child, would you let me attend your schools, would you welcome me into your homes? Or would you look at me as if I were a stray dog, and kick me away?'

Once, as a child of six, she'd stared longingly through a classroom window. Now, ignoring the pain in her foot, she jumped on the memory of the caretaker who'd chased her from the playground.

'When you look at me, what do you see?' her shoes clacked as she approached the crowd in a stamping fury. The tourists drew back, laughing and clapping. 'Do you see Rosalita, a woman with brains, a talent for telling stories, a thirst for knowledge? Or am I just a doll in a pretty dress who spins around for you?'

Startled, sensing the dancer was subverting the ritual, the crowd roared, their applause threatening and raw. The musicians continued their refrain, increasing the volume as if to protect Rosalita from the baying crowd. Their presence sheltered her, suffocated her. She whirled again towards her family, banging her feet.

'And you!' she glared, holding her pose for a moment before kicking out. 'Do you just see a girl who is only good for cooking, for begging, for childminding, for washing your dirty clothes? A woman you only let out to dance for these people who despise us?'

Her skirt was heavy with sweat, dragging her down. The night was a hot velvet cloak, stiflingly beautiful. Tiredly, the guitarists strummed on.

"*Que dice la zarzamora?*" lamented Elmita. "*Que pena tengo en mi corazon...*" Her voice was growing hoarse – she darted an appealing glance at Rosalita. "*No tengo libertad en mi vida.*"

Rosalita danced on in a trance of pain.

She would not stop, she would dance forever beneath these sequin stars, this golden moon, whirling and twirling and swirling in an eternal prayer of freedom. Because if she stopped, she'd have to ease the scuffed red shoe off her blistered foot, and release her throbbing bunion.

Glossary

Dios – Lord   (Spanish)

payos – term used by Spanish Gypsies to describe non-Gypsies

Calí – term which some Spanish Gypsies use to describe themselves

Gitana/Gitanos – Gypsy/Gypsies   (Spanish)

zarzamora – blackberry   (Spanish)

barrio – area   (Spanish)

palmas – hand claps   (Spanish)

llamada – signal to guitarist that dancer wants to begin dance, or start new sequence of steps   (Spanish)

redoble – heel beats   (Spanish)

caretilla – a continuous roll of castanets   (Spanish)

Cuba libre – a drink made of cola, lime, and white rum (literally 'Free Cuba')   (Spanish)

"Que dice la zarzamora?" – "what does the blackberry say?" (Spanish)

"Que pena tengo en mi corazon" – "What pain I have in my heart" (Spanish)

"No tengo libertad en mi vida" – "I have no freedom in my life" (Spanish)

The Konsat

<u>friday july 22. My first diary writing about konsat in last day of</u>
<u>term.</u>

I am going English class every day. My teacher is saying I am doing very good. For me is not to hard too learning langwijs, while i have been living always in different places in my live. And teacher sujest all student writing diary in English on long summer holiday, so nobody not forgotting the English langwij. This my entrant about our konsat today. Last day of term konsat.

Teacher say tell diary first who are you. So I start on me. My name is Teresa, my family is Gypsies. I am coming with little sister Ruzhe since two year ago from Romania. Actually I born Jugoslavia, then there is coming war, so we are running into German. But are many bads problems in German, so later we running in Hungary, then Romania. But this is even more worse, so we coming England.

All refugees in my class. Running from differents countries. Sometimes I think hole world is running from one place to the other place. Crazy. My friend in class is Sandi she is coming from the Zimbabwe. Before I not knowing where is the Zimbabwe, but Sandi show me on the big carte sticking on wall in classroom. She is telling me all her family have been dead. They dead becoz wrong tribe. This is terrible, like situation for us Roma in Yugoslavia or German. If you are Gypsy with black hair and dark face, people not liking you. In Romania they calling Gypsies blackbirds, saying we are black. Sandi is more blacker than me. – No, Teresa – Sandi say me, – you are not black. *I* am black. – She putting her arm on my arm and she is rite – she is black and i am brown.

Is nice in my kollij. Everyday we having class, I am in top class. I am sitting next one man from Iran, kwite rich man, but always he crying. Becoz his wife has been dead. She is not wanting to ware this *hijab* – hijab is like *diklo* for Roma woman. And his wife put in prison and cach the TB and dye. This terrible thing. In Jugoslavia I to am wearing this hijab, but in England I not wearing. Only on church or in special days.

Today we make konsat. End of term konsat. End of summer term. For one month everyone is making practiss. Parviz, the rich crying man of Iran, he is drumming on *davulka*. He makes very good drumming, rembring me for my brother Dušan. Dušan he make always

90

the drums in partis and weding. He is very talent. Now he is dead.
Never may I too understand why people like to killing other people just
becoz they Roma or from wrong tribe in the Zimbabwe. Or for not
wearing *diklo* in Iran. Is very strange to me.

Another frend is coming from China. Called disa dent. Not
agreeing with government. Her name calls Mei. In konsat Mei doing
singing. Is very sweet and very very high, like *cirikili*. I look this
word in dictionery. Like lark. My mother always is singing like lark
before my father dyes. Later she is stopping singing as very sad.
Father getting very ill one winter, always coffin but doctor not coming
to our vilij. "Me no coming at Roma vilij – bad people," doctor is
saying. We got no money for doctor, but even for rich Roma in vilij
sometime doctor no coming. Roma not deserving doctor, this what
some people say.

So today end day of term. Everyone must bringing some thing for
eat from their country. Parviz bringing *baklava*. Buyun bringing
burek. Cahit bringing kebab. Dapika bringing hot kurri. I bringing
zumi, this mean a soup. I bringing in flask and put on table. We
drinking from cups and Sandi say – very nice your soup. Say me how
you making it.

First is konsat. I am thinking will be luvly, but actually is not so
luvly. I no no why. Peeple laffing wen not very funy. Example.
Parviz playing drum, and I playing rekorda. We playing at same time.
I think is very luvly. Teechers think is very luvly, but Curdy boys
laffing.

Next thing, Mei singing, very high. Curdy boys laffing agen.
Parviz smiling also like he think is funny. Mei finish song but looking
upset. Why this boys are laffing? Teecher gives bad look and boys
laffing more louder.

Next Abdul saying pome. First saying in Arabi, and Curdy boys
laffing. Then Abdul translateing to English, and boys no lissening. I
look at teecher to tell off, but she just looking at Abdul and smiling.
Then clapping. Abdul looking sadly becoz boys rudeness.

Now is turn of Curdy boys. Tarik putting on CD, but Mohamet
take off. Mohamet say, – no no no this not rite musika! – Curdy boys
having discushion about musika. I look Abdul and Parviz and Mei and
Dipika. We starting laffing. Laffing very loud. No body looking at
Curdy boys. They dansing in sirkel. Really is very nice dansing and I
want to dans also, but I laffing too much. Is good for Curdy boys to
lern evry has rite to there musika and singing. No matter if diffrent
from your musika. At last boys stamping and clapping and we

stopping laffing and join sirkel. This is betta. Is very nice all difrent peopel together.

Now we eating. Parviz upset agen for Agneta sitting on *davulka*. This big *davulka* look like seat but is drum. "This very much money in my country," say Parviz. "Please get up from *davulka* and sit on chair."

I hungry. I sitting by window and eating. In my kultur not polite to look wen people eating. First eating, then talking. In this country everybody eating and talking at same time, you can see in their mouth. Not nice. Mama always say me, eat and not talk, so Shatan don't get in body. This Shatan like England devil. We always eat qwick, in case cum truble. Mama say this custom from since old long long ago ages time, when Roma live in tents, and polis coming to tell go away.

In Yugoslavia we live in house. In German we live in hostel but in Romania we live in old old cabin now burn down. I try not remember that nite, but is like burn in my head. First we here noise from down road, like singing. But not nise singing. Angry singing. Coming neerer and neerer, hearing words. – Go, Gypsies. Leave us in piece. Leave our town. Go away Gypsies. Go bak your country. Go before we making fire smoke.

Qwick qwik Mama rapping baby in shorl. I take Ruzhe, we run. Ware we go. I not thinking. Just go qwick. This next bit so hard for riting. Just to say me and Ruzhe alone now live. All other familia ded. Burn.

This why we come England. Me and Ruzhe. Ruzhe nine, now go skool. Kleva girl but always cry. Always sad. I cuming this collij, finish learn English. Next get good job and by house. Now liv in shelter for the Asylum Seekers. Is here many peeple from many country, all running, running. Hole world just running.

Is funny. I living in London, but in my airia not many England people. In lokal shop is India man, in soupamarkt is Malawi and Irak peeple. Wun day wen teecha invite class to kaff, Poland people make coffee, and Agneta becoming very exciting and start talking coffee peoples very kwick. We suprize becoz in class Agneta always kwite kwite.

In Ruzhe skool lot of children talking Poland or Turkey or Curdy or China. Sumtime inviting her to home. Nais peeple. We shy invite them to our hostel for not pretty, to much peeple, sometime kichen not kleen enuff. We Roma very worry about kleen. We have one bol for body wash, different bols for plates wash, more bols for clothes wash. And always kichen very kleen. We call bad name for dirty peeple.

This enuff I rite today diary. I think important lesson from konsat. We must lisening each other and lerning from each other. This Roma way. Travel world and here different musika, look different dansing. Taking musika from one place to another place. This is luvly thing Roma peeple do. Not sit on peeple drum. Not laffing at different style. Appreshiate everything.

This is meaning from konsat.

Glossary

Hijab – head covering worn by Muslim women   (Arabic)

diklo – scarf   (*Romani*)

burek – filo pasties   (Turkish)

Essex Girl

"I won't go to school today, Mammie!"

Breed stood her ground as her mother walked heavily towards her.

"Stop your nonsense, Breed! You will so! Shift yourself now!"

Breed twisted a lock of hair round her finger, pulling till it hurt. As always, the pain calmed her down.

She stared up at her mother's freckled red face. "Martin and Maggie don't have to go to school. They've never been. They're older than me, but their Mammie lets them stay home and help her. I could help you. I'll clean the windows and air the bedding. I'll bake ....."

"Wheesht with your nonsense! That feckless Rona McCartney, she hasn't a care in the world, but I want more for you, my girl. I want you to have a better life than me and your da."

Breed tried to squirm away from her mother's arms, but she was marched into the bedroom and forced into her uniform. "There!" Mammie said, fastening the top button of Breed's dress. "Now, tidy your hair, and you'll be ready to go."

"I'm not going!" Breed insisted. "You've no right to make me. It's against the law!"

Mammie sat down heavily on the bed. "Against the law is it? And what do you know about laws? Fix your hair now while you give me an answer."

Sullenly Breed tugged the comb through her hair, wincing as the prongs dug into her scalp. A scream burst out of her mouth and turned into a loud sob. Tears rolled down her face.

Her mother's arms were round her, soft and firm, pulling her onto her lap. "Whatever's the matter, darlin'? Are you being bullied at that school now, is that what it is?"

"No, it's not that. Most of the kids are nice. It's just that Suresh told me ....."

She stopped. What Suresh had said was too awful to repeat.

"Go on."

"His daddy works for the Council. And Jenny's mam's a social worker. And they said that all the kids on our site will be taken into care. They said the social will come to the school and get us. So I can't go to school, do ye see, Mammie. The Council will take me away while I'm in class, and you won't know where I am. Please, Mammie, you have to let me stay home!"

Mammie stiffened, as if someone had jabbed her on an old injury. "That's the way of it, is it? Come on now! We'll go and see Uncle Richard. He'll know what to do."

Breed's heart slowed to its normal rhythm and she wiped her eyes. Uncle Richard was the leader of the Travellers on their site. He'd sort everything out. Everyone respected Uncle Richard; even the local councillors. He'd seen troublemakers off before, like those journalists who'd written horrible things about their site in the press.

She tugged at a curl, wincing as the hair came out at the root. "I don't understand what all the fuss is about, Mammie," she said. "Isn't it grand living where we know everyone? I like having Auntie Mary and Uncle Johnnie just across the way. Can you believe Hakim's relations live far off in Birmingham and Pakistan, and Jenny lives on her own with her mam?"

She stared out of the window at the well-kept garden. "Why would anyone want to close us down?"

The troubles had got worse after the builders put up a wooden shed on some spare land near Auntie May's trailer. "A Community Centre," Richard had told Breed's Da over a cup of tea one day. "For the youngsters to learn the computers, for us adults to have meetings and run courses, a place for celebrations and the like."

Breed had heard Mammie say some local villagers were complaining because the site residents hadn't got something called planning permission. But the builders had finished the shed anyway.

Breed was one of the children chosen to perform at the opening of the Community Centre. She'd read out a story, and her brother Sean had danced a jig. Some famous people had visited that day. A man called Lord Avebury cut the ceremonial ribbon and gave the opening speech. Breed had been a bit disappointed when she saw him. She thought Lords wore red robes and long white wigs, but this Lord was in corduroy trousers and hadn't even got on a tie. "Call me Eric," he said to everyone.

He was a grand talker though, and a supporter of the Travellers. In his speech, he said that the threat of site closure was short-sighted, as evictions would pose economic and social problems. "Too many long words," Sean had complained, running off to play in the sunshine with his puppy. Breed had stayed to listen though, recording the speech on her mobile. She liked to collect long words to use for homework and answering questions in class.

Breed often repeated the closing phrases of Eric's speech to herself so she wouldn't forget them. "If this site is closed, the children, at present well integrated into local schools, will become the expensive responsibility of emergency Social Services. My message to the local Council is, "Don't do it! Don't damage Britain's reputation for tolerance!"

Everyone had clapped really loudly at that bit, then Father John blessed the wooden building with Holy Water, and all the Travellers and the visitors had a bite to eat. There'd been sandwiches and juice and beer, and Auntie Helen brought out the loudspeaker from her trailer and played country and western music. The women sat on chairs in the sunshine, and some people got up and danced. It was a gas.

One of the journalists had talked to Breed's Nan. "I don't know what will become of us if we're thrown off the site," Nan told the reporter, her face lined with tiredness. "I'm too old to go back on the road."

When Nan said that, Breed felt really frightened. Were they really going to close her beautiful site, the place where she'd lived most of her life. Would she really have to move away and leave her school friends behind?

That's when she'd begun pulling at her curls, tugging hair from her head. The sharp pain soothed her. Winding the red strands round her fingers and rolling them into tiny balls helped dull the worry. Flicking the balls of hair away, she imagined she was throwing off all her sorrow.

"Ready?" Mammie asked. "We'll see what Uncle Richard thinks about the Social putting yous into care."

Richard's trailer was just across the way. Breed stared at the beautiful statuette of Our Lady of Grace on the shelf, and pictures of the Bleeding Heart on the walls.

"Tell Uncle Richard what your little friends said," ordered Mam.

Breed took a ringlet in her hand, and pulled her hair. Then she looked at Uncle Richard. She felt important, like a councillor at a meeting. Like a Lord in Parliament.

"Suresh is in my class. His daddy works in the Council. And he heard that all the children living here will be put into care if the site's closed. Suresh says we must run away."

"No one's running away!" Uncle Richard said. His face was white and his eyes looked cross and sad at the same time. "They never chased us off Cherry Orchard, and they won't chase us off now!"

Breed knew the legend of Cherry Orchard. It was a story the old folk told of an evening, or after a baptism or confirmation. It had happened a long time ago, way back in the last century, somewhere in Ireland, near Dublin. In those times, the Travelling People had been persecuted and chased from one county to another. After being moved around for years on end, the Travellers were ill, tired and hungry. And at last, when they'd camped up in Cherry Orchard, there'd been a big fight, and the authorities had backed down.

"Aye!" Uncle Richard said. "That was the day us Travelling People won a great victory. And we'll fight again if we have to. We've too much to lose."

Breed smiled. There was nothing to worry about. They would fight and win and stay in their lovely home just off the winding Essex lane for ever and ever.

She would go back to school tomorrow. They were learning about the Holocaust and the fight for equality and justice. About discrimination and the way minorities had been massacred during the Second World War. That was way back in the last century too, like the battle of Cherry Orchard.

"Some of them Cherry Orchard parents put their children in front of the bulldozers," Uncle Richard went on. Breed noticed his eyes had gone all misty, like the Irish hills he was always blathering on about. "Me own Da stuck *me* in front of one of them bulldozers too! I remember the machine swinging around, the driver hanging onto the joystick for dear life. "We'll not hurt the little children," said the workers, and they threw down their tools and left the field. Aye, that was a great victory!"

"Stop pulling at your hair now, Breed," said Mammie. "You'll be bald before you're eleven if you keep on!"

Other books by Janna

Settela's Last Road Historical novel Trafford Publications 2008

Spokes Collection of short stories with a *Romani* spin Five Leaves
Publications 2008

The Magic Stones, The Two Brothers, Tasty Stone Soup *Romani* poem
tales for children 2010

Translations by Janna

Settela by Aad Wagenaar Five Leaves Publications 2005

Sofia Z-4515 by Gunilla Lundgren Mantra Lingua Publications 2012

CPSIA information can be obtained at www.ICGtesting.com
Printed in the USA
LVOW05s1710221113

362439LV00001B/199/P